WHERE THE KILLER LURKED...

After the first dry crack of the pistol splintered wood from the edge of the buckboard seat, Lark reacted instantly. Gripping his rifle firmly, he leaped to the ground. "Get out of here!" he shouted at Charity. "And don't stop 'til you get to Loven's place!"

As Charity Gunderson whipped the old bay into a lumbering run, Lark caught the crackle of dry branches immediately ahead of him. He threw himself to his right instinctively, expecting a second shot by the bushwhacker. None came. Suspicious, wondering, he rushed headlong into the springy growth, striving frantically to get a glimpse of the killer.

Nothing. No sound of anyone running, no sign of movement. Lark halted, breathing hard, stifling his raspy gasps to listen. But it was as if he were utterly alone in the universe. . . .

Signet Brand Western

GUN TRAP AT ARABELLA

◎ ◎ ◎ ◎ ◎ ◎ ◎ ◎

by
Ray Hogan

A SIGNET BOOK
NEW AMERICAN LIBRARY
TIMES MIRROR

NAL BOOKS ARE ALSO AVAILABLE AT DISCOUNTS IN BULK QUANTITY FOR INDUSTRIAL OR SALES-PROMOTIONAL USE. FOR DETAILS, WRITE TO PREMIUM MARKETING DIVISION, NEW AMERICAN LIBRARY, INC., 1301 AVENUE OF THE AMERICAS, NEW YORK, NEW YORK 10019.

SIGNET TRADEMARK REG. U.S. PAT. OFF. AND FOREIGN COUNTRIES
REGISTERED TRADEMARK—MARCA REGISTRADA
HECHO EN CHICAGO, U.S.A.

SIGNET, SIGNET CLASSICS, MENTOR, PLUME AND MERIDIAN BOOKS
are published by The New American Library, Inc.,
1301 Avenue of the Americas, New York, New York 10019

FIRST SIGNET PRINTING, FEBRUARY, 1978

1 2 3 4 5 6 7 8 9

PRINTED IN THE UNITED STATES OF AMERICA

◎ 1 ◎

"Five men dead! Murdered—shot down in cold blood!" the governor stormed. "And you haven't done a damned thing about it!"

John Foreman, wearing a gold-plated sheriff's star rather than the customary silver, brushed at the sweat on his forehead with the back of a hand. It was August and the summer heat locked Kingdom City in a viselike grip.

"I've done what I could," the lawman said defensively. "Went down there to Arabella, tried to get to the bottom of it. Had to leave—"

"You've got to go there and stay!" the governor snapped irritably. "Only way you'll run down this killer, whoever he is."

"I realize that, but I can't do it," Foreman said. Although he was far from comfortable in his gray whipcord suit and white shirt closed at the throat with a black string tie, he was pleased to have the governor, paying an unexpected visit, find him looking his best.

"Like to know why?"

"My county covers close to seven thousand square miles—and Arabella's not the only town in it—"

"I know how big it is, and I'll admit the law's spread mighty thin all over the territory, but we've still got a job to do—all of us."

"I've got other towns to look after," Foreman continued doggedly. "And the fall court term's coming soon. That'll tie me down all the more. Cahoon there'll tell you that a man can only do so much without help."

Hazen Langley, a slim, dark, intense man, had been the territory governor for two years and was looking ahead to a repeat term if he could maintain what was generally considered to be a good administration. But the murders that had occurred at Arabella, or nearby, were rapidly becoming a scandal, which was fuel for the opposing political party, and he'd made the long trip down from the capital to talk to John Foreman and see what could be done about it. Frowning, he glanced at Deputy U.S. Marshal Jesse Cahoon, who was leaning against a wall and listening without comment.

Cahoon, a small, wiry man in his forties, shrugged. He had dark, quick eyes and a stillness to him that men found disturbing.

"Sheriff's right, Governor," he drawled. Sweat was standing in beads on the flat planes of his weathered face, too, but he seemed not to notice. "Territory can sure use more lawmen."

Langley swore softly at a fact he was fully aware of, turned, looked out into the street. Kingdom City was a busy town despite its not being one of the larger settlements. At that hour, even in the driving heat, quite a few people were on the board sidewalks, and the flow of buggies, wagons, and riders on horseback was constant.

"What about your deputies? Have you sent one down there?"

"Two—all I've got," Foreman said. "First one just dropped out of sight—rode off and never came back. I don't know what happened."

"You said he rode off—you know that for certain?"

"Well, no, not exactly, but that seemed to be—"

"Then he could be the sixth man murdered down there," the governor said heavily.

Foreman nodded slowly. "Got that idea myself, but I couldn't turn up any evidence of it while I was there."

"What about the other deputy? You said two—"

"Name's Morgan. Other'n was Norm Louis. I'm not sure what happened to Morgan. Was found at the bottom of a bluff—arm and leg broken. Claims his horse threw him. He's still laid up."

Hazen Langley sighed. "So what's next? I don't want to have to send the militia down there, put the town under martial law. Be a black eye to me and the administration, and to you, too."

"Aim to send another deputy soon as he reports for work," Foreman said. Slim, neat, his carriage reflected the military career he'd abandoned for one in politics when the war was over.

"That be today—tomorrow?"

"A few days. Hired a man who's working for the sheriff in Denver. Plenty of experience and—"

Langley impatiently waved the lawman to silence, swung his attention to Cahoon. "Any chance you can give us a little help in this, Marshal? Maybe you could ride down to Arabella, see what you can turn up. You might even be able to nail that killer before he murders somebody else."

Jesse Cahoon shook his head. "Sure sorry, Governor. Ain't nothing I'd like better, but I've got business over on the east side of the territory that's got to be tended to, and with the marshal down sick, there's a dozen other things he wants me to look after."

Langley moved slowly to the doorway of Foreman's stuffy, heat-filled office, stared unseeingly at the passersby. After a few moments he wheeled to the lawman, his face stern, almost drawn.

"You've got to do something, John—and do it damned quick! These doings at Arabella are hurting me bad, and they'll hurt you plenty too. You've built yourself a good record so far, and there could be bigger things ahead for you, but your failure to get anything done down there could ruin you. Expect you know words finally reached the newspapers about it and they're starting to play it up big."

Again Foreman swiped at the sweat on his face. The thought of all his political hopes going down into dust brought a worried frown to his features and set his mouth to a grim line. He'd thrown in with Langley and his party immediately after leaving the army. The choice had been a good one; Hazen Langley was a comer, likely would rise to a seat in the U.S. Senate one day, and all those who had supported and assisted him in his climb would benefit accordingly.

John Foreman had set the governor's chair as his goal, and by cherishing the right friends and cultivating the proper connections he knew he could make it if something didn't happen to foul him up—things like the five mysterious murders at

Arabella, or to be more exact, at Arabella Lake, which was near the settlement.

"This new man from Denver—any chance of getting him down here sooner?"

Foreman ran a finger around the inside of his collar, grimaced. "Talked to him about it—told him I was needing him bad. Said he couldn't pull out and leave the sheriff up there flat, that he'd have to wait until a man could be hired to replace him."

Strain was showing in Hazen Langley's eyes. "Well, what about the town marshal at Crawfordsville—or some of the other sheriffs?"

"All too busy—tied up. They've got court going into session in their counties, too, and that marshal at Crawfordsville, he's nothing more'n a constable looking after the jail. Wouldn't be no help."

"Like as not wouldn't come anyway," Cahoon said. "Nobody wants to become dead man number six down there."

The governor shrugged helplessly, flicked a speck of dust from the sleeve of his tailored suit with a fingernail. "Appears I'm no better off for coming down here than if I'd stayed in my office at the capital," he said in a resigned sort of way. "I don't know any more about the situation than I did, and you can't give me any positive assurance that you'll be doing something about Arabella anytime soon. I regret that."

Langley paused, allowed his words to register fully on Foreman. A clever man who orated even when he was having a face-to-face conversation with a friend, he was a natural politician and knew how to handle subordinates and get the most out of them—only too often by sly innuendo.

"Looks to me as if I have no alternative but to

step in, send down the militia. Means I'll be putting a big club in the hands of the opposition party, and ruining a few promising careers, but something has to be done or—"

John Foreman straightened suddenly, crossed to the window. Halting there, as Langley broke off, frowning, he centered his attention on a rider moving slowly by. Both Cahoon and the governor, puzzled, followed the lawman's line of sight.

Langley said: "What is it?"

"It's him sure'n hell," Foreman muttered, and without turning, added, "Governor, maybe—just maybe—I've got the answer to our problem."

"You mean that saddlebum going by?" Cahoon asked, squinting at the rag-tag figure in faded, worn clothing slumped on the saddle of a tired-looking buckskin horse. "You saying he's the answer?"

"That saddlebum, if I'm not wrong, is Lark Prestridge," Foreman said. "He was a sergeant in my outfit during the war—First Missouri Cavalry. He's one hell of a man—or was, and I don't reckon he's changed. A real sharpshooter with a rifle and just about as good with a pistol—and what's more, he's the kind with more guts than good sense."

Langley was following the rider's progress along the street. He read the lawman's mind. "You're thinking to hire him, send him down to Arabella as a deputy—"

Foreman nodded. "Wouldn't have to wait on that man from Denver—and if there's anybody around who can get to the bottom of the trouble in Arabella, it's Prestridge."

"Hire him," Langley said abruptly, decisively. "Pay him whatever he wants. If you need funds, call on my office."

"From the looks of him," Cahoon said, stroking his mustache, "I'd say you could get him for a square meal and a bottle of whiskey."

"Don't judge him yet—there's many a man's been down on his luck," Foreman said. "And if he's the Lark Prestridge I knew in the war, he'll be worth any price."

Hazen Langley picked up his hat, creased it carefully and placed it on his head at just the proper angle. "I'll leave it up to you, John," he said, moving toward the doorway. "I think you've got the right idea if this man's as good as you claim. . . . I'll expect to hear from you in a couple of days."

"It'll take more than a couple of days to get him down to Arabella!" Foreman said protestingly.

"Yeh, guess you're right. Make it a week. If you haven't sent word to me by then that you've got a man on the job, I'll have no option other than to send in the militia—and you know what that could do to both our careers."

The sheriff nodded. "Prestridge'll get the job done—I'll lay odds on it."

"Sounds fine—and I'll rely on you," Langley said, stepping out onto the landing that fronted the lawman's quarters. Hesitating, he looked back questioningly at Cahoon. "You going my way, Marshal?"

Cahoon said, "No, I'm waiting for Ed Wheeler from the Land Office. He's bringing some papers he wants me to drop off in Junction Center when I go by. Besides, I want to hang around, get a gander at this ring-tailed wonder Foreman's bragging up. Man just don't run into them kind much any more."

"For sure," the governor said, and moved on.

2

Lark Prestridge rode slowly down the hot, dusty street, eyes squinted to cut down the glare, taking in the people along the walks, the store buildings beyond them, the coming and going of vehicles and horsemen around him. Kingdom City, the sign at the fork in the road had said; it wasn't a bad little town, he noted—but then he reckoned any town was all right if a man could find work there.

Much time had passed since Appomattox, and he still hadn't turned up a decent job—not in the dozen states or territories he'd drifted through. *Times are hard;* those were the words that he'd encountered everywhere, and he had no reason to doubt it. Just as Reconstruction, which applied to the secession states, was at a standstill, so also was postwar recovery in most all others.

And it made no difference which color uniform a man had worn during the war—there just wasn't any call for one whose expertise was limited to the use of a Henry repeating rifle and a converted cap-and-ball Colt pistol.

But somewhere he guessed he'd find a job that he'd fit into, one that would enable him to start a life that had never really begun. He wasn't giving up. There was a niche somewhere for every man, he'd heard said, so he reckoned it was just a matter of looking until he found his.

Arizona, the newly created territory, offered possibility. Mining was booming, so rumor had it, and he might find work riding shotgun for ore wagons, and if not that, well, he wasn't above swinging a pick and shovel if there was nothing else—for a while. He'd done a little of everything from sweeping out saloons and forking manure in stables on up, so if necessary, fitting his hands to a pick handle would be no big problem.

But Arizona was still a far piece away, and busy as Kingdom City appeared to be, it would be smart to ask about employment. He was in cattle country, although in passing he had also noted many homesteads in the lower valleys; he could turn in a reasonable day's work at either, but if there was a preference he would choose the former. Even something temporary would be welcome. He was next to being stone broke.

Prestridge lifted his head, let his glance search along the storefronts for a saloon. Bartenders were always good ones to talk to, he'd learned; they knew about everything that was said, rumored or thought of and could usually be relied upon to supply all the information a man needed to know concerning a town.

The Silver Star looked promising. It stood on the corner just ahead, was fairly large and apparently enjoyed a good amount of business. He'd try there, Lark decided, and slanted the buckskin he was riding toward a hitch rack erected at the side of the building.

Pulling up abreast the other horses standing at the rack, Prestridge swung down and wrapped the gelding's lines around the crossbar. He straightened up then, remained motionless in the driving sunlight as if allowing the muscles of his lank body to adjust after many hours in the saddle. Finally, pivoting unhurriedly, he drew his rifle from its boot, stepped up onto the saloon's landing and crossed to its open doorway.

Entering, Lark halted briefly to glance about the shadowy interior, and then moved toward the long bar that he could see against the opposite wall. There weren't many patrons, at least in the saloon itself, and he reckoned the riders of the horses outside were elsewhere in the building gambling, perhaps, or enjoying the company of the women provided by the management.

Nodding to the half-dozen men who were present and strung out along the counter, Lark faced the bartender, a squat, dark-haired man with a waxed mustache.

"Beer."

"Big or little?"

Prestridge had never been asked that before. He shrugged. "Little, I reckon. Whatever a nickel'll buy."

The man behind the bar pulled back, drew a small glass of foaming liquid from a keg, placed it in front of Lark and waited expectantly. Leaning his rifle against his leg, Prestridge selected the proper coin from his slim reserve and handed it to the man.

"Any place around here where a man can find himself a job?" he asked.

"Nope," the bartender said immediately with a shake of his head.

Prestridge studied the man coldly. "You sure didn't give a hell of a lot of thought to it. Suppose you think again."

The saloonman frowned, stiffened. Abruptly his expression changed as he caught the look in Lark Prestridge's hard-surfaced gray eyes.

"Well, now, I don't know," he began hurriedly. "I maybe—"

"If you're busted I'll buy that rifle you're toting," the first man in the line along the counter offered.

Prestridge shifted his attention to the speaker, a rancher, judging by his clothing. Lark shook his head. There's been offers made before to buy the Henry repeater, and he'd turned them all down regardless of the price quoted. It had been his faithful companion during the last year of the war, and when the fighting was over, the colonel commanding the cavalry brigade to which he was attached had presented it to him in lieu of the medal he felt was due Lark.

"Obliged, but it's not for sale," he said.

"Always wanted me one of them Henry .44's," the rancher said, setting his glass on the counter and moving over to Prestridge. "Plenty scarce around here—most other places, too. Fellows that've got one just ain't interested in parting with it. . . . Mind if I have me a look at yours?"

Lark gave it a moment's thought, shifted the pistol on his hip forward slightly, and said: "Go ahead."

The rancher reached down, brought the rifle up

to chest level. His drinking companions edged in for a closer view.

"She's in fine shape," the man said, examining the worn but well-cared-for weapon admiringly. "Can see you ain't abused her none."

Prestridge nodded. A tall man in a light suit looking on said, "One of the first models. Magazine fills from the muzzle end."

"Best way, no matter what some folks thinks," the rancher declared. "Can load up fast."

"All in what suits a fellow, I reckon," the tall man replied indifferently and rapped on the bar to get attention. "Fill me up again, Pete," he said and moved back to his original place. As the others followed him, the rancher reluctantly propped the rifle against the front of the counter next to Prestridge.

"There ain't no chance of you changing your mind about selling?" he asked hopefully.

"None," Lark said and turned to his glass of beer. "Don't figure I'll ever get hungry enough to—"

His words broke off as his glance settled on a figure coming through the doorway. He swore silently. The law—a sheriff. Lark knew what he could now expect—questions as to who he was, where he came from and where he was going, how long he'd be in town, and such. Like as not his answers would fail to satisfy the lawman and he'd be told to be on his way by sundown. There was a time when he'd stood up to the town marshals and sheriffs and refused to be bullied by them—but it didn't matter all that much any more.

The rancher was saying something about the Henry as he moved away, but Prestridge was not listening. His attention was, instead, on the lawman, well dressed and approaching with a smile. There was something vaguely familiar to the man.

"Sergeant?" the sheriff said as he drew near.

Recognition came to Lark Prestridge at the word. It was John Foreman, a captain he'd served under during the war.

3

Foreman, all smiles and radiating friendliness, came forward with arm extended. Nodding crisply to the men at the bar, he halted before Prestridge.

"Sure surprised to see you here in my town, Lark!" he said heartily, grasping Prestridge's hand before it was even offered, and pumping it vigorously. "Been close to three years since we rode together. How've things been for you?"

It was an unnecessary question, Lark thought. Foreman had only to look at him and have his answer, but he smiled wryly, shrugged.

"Good enough, I reckon."

The star John Foreman wore was gold-plated, Lark noted. That was typical of the man; he'd not be content with the nickel or silver badges other lawmen used; he'd have to go them one better.

Foreman had drawn back a step, was surveying Prestridge admiringly. "Want you all to know who this man is," he said, sweeping the patrons at the bar with his glance. "Name's Lark Prestridge

—and for my money he's the bravest man I've ever met!"

Lark, frowning, took a swallow of his beer, conscious of the close attention now being paid him.

"Fact is," Foreman continued, "I owe him my life, same as does four other men who happened to be with me one day during the war. Was at a place called Sugar Creek."

The lawman paused. Lark stirred uncomfortably, again sipped at his beer. A tall, lean man with cool eyes and a square-cut face halved by a full mustache, he looked to be in need of everything—from a shave and a trim of his dark hair to a change of clothing, beginning with the scarred, flat-heeled Hyers on his feet and ending with the ragged-brimmed army campaign hat on his head.

"What'd he do, Sheriff?" the bartender asked in a tone that indicated he was finding it difficult to believe one so nondescript could possibly be a hero.

"Saved my hide and that of four soldiers," Foreman replied promptly. "We were engaged with the enemy. It was a fierce scrimmage and I suddenly found myself—I was one of the brigade captains—pinned down in a little coulee with the men I mentioned. The enemy was all around us, and it sure looked like the war was all over for us.

"Then I saw Sergeant Prestridge coming toward us, crawling through the tall grass. He reached us somehow without being spotted, and then, using his repeater rifle, covered our retreat. Happens he's a sharpshooter—one of the best I've ever seen. If he hadn't been I doubt if me or any of those boys would've got out of there alive."

Several of the men at the counter nodded approvingly. Foreman made the affair sound like a lot more than it actually was—and if the truth were known, Lark thought, remembering—he was going after the enlisted men, who were friends of his, when he started across the field that morning, and not John Foreman. He had never cared much for the officer, and it was only a coincidence that he was rescued along with the others.

"You get a medal of some kind for that, Sergeant?" asked the rancher who had wanted to buy the Henry.

"No, he didn't," Foreman answered quickly. "I put in for one but it never came through. Did see that he got to keep his rifle, though, as a sort of a reward."

Lark Prestridge studied his empty glass. That was the first he'd heard of Foreman having anything to do with his getting the Henry. It had been Colonel Cleveland who had told him the weapon was his; the colonel had added that he believed it small compensation for the fine job Lark had done for his country. Anyway, a lot of men hung onto their guns when the war ended, although there had been an effort by the War Department to recover the special weapons.

"Told Lark at the time that I owed him," Foreman continued. "Said that if ever I could do him a favor, no matter what, he had only to look me up."

Prestridge did not look up from his glass. He'd long since forgotten John Foreman's having said that, but the words came back to him now. He had to be honest about it all, however.

"Recollect you saying that, all right, but I never came here looking for you. Truth is I didn't know where you were. Just happened to be passing through on my way to Arizona."

"Just proves there's something to this thing folks call fate!" Foreman said. "You're needing a job, I take it, and I can use a good man."

Lark came to attention, considered the lawman through narrowing eyes. Foreman was offering him work. Suspicion rose quickly within Prestridge; unless John Foreman had changed considerably any favors he extended had best be viewed with caution.

"You interested?" he heard the lawman ask.

"Depends," Lark answered. "What kind of a job?"

"Deputy—actually a special deputy. Can't promise you it'll be permanent, but if things work out right—"

"That trouble down at Arabella—that what you're hirin' 'im to look into?" one of the saloon patrons wondered.

Foreman frowned. "Possibly," he said, and nodded to Lark. "You like to talk about it? If so, let's go set at a table where there won't be somebody butting in. . . . Harry, bring us a bottle and a couple of glasses," he added to the bartender, and without waiting for Prestridge to make a reply, cut away from the bar and crossed to a table some distance from it.

Prestridge delayed briefly, reluctant to become beholden to a man for whom he had no respect, but a job was a job and he reckoned that as long as it paid cash money, he'd best at least consider it. Rising, he trailed the lawman to the table and sat down opposite.

Foreman waited until the bartender had provided the bottle of whiskey and the necessary glasses, and then, pouring drinks, he leaned forward.

"Job's a tough one," he said. "Won't try fooling you on that, but I know the kind of man you are, and I figure if anybody can handle it, you can. Told the governor as much."

Lark smiled faintly. Then, "Arabella—that's a town around here somewhere?"

"Yeh, south of here, in my county. There's a lake nearby, same name. Been five murders down there—coldblooded killings. Nobody has any idea who did it—or why. The town's in a panic. Folks are afraid to stir about, leave their homes."

Lark studied his drink silently. He hadn't enjoyed a shot of good whiskey in weeks, was savoring it. Abruptly he lifted the glass, tossed off the liquor in a single gulp. Setting the glass down, he raised his level glance to John Foreman.

"Have you been down there looking into it?"

"Of course I have!" the lawman said, his voice rising slightly. "My job to."

Prestridge considered that for a few moments. Maybe he was misjudging Foreman; maybe his onetime captain, who had been known in the army as a man filled with personal ambition, had changed.

"You didn't turn up anything?"

"Nope, not a damn thing!" Foreman said, taking a sip of his whiskey. "Talked to everybody I could, and none of them could tell me anything except there'd been five killings—three homesteaders and two hired hands—all at different times."

"Got to be a reason for it."

"I couldn't come up with one. That's what's got me stumped. Why were the men murdered? Sent two deputies down there, too. One of them just up and pulled out. Don't know why—and I couldn't find anybody in Arabella, either the town or at the homesteads around the lake, who could give me an answer."

Lark helped himself to another drink. "You said two deputies—"

"Coming to the other one. Horse threw him. Broke him up pretty good. I don't think it had anything to do with the killer."

"No lawman in the town?"

"No. Place is too little. Always had to look after things there myself. Same all over the territory. Towns come to life, maybe a couple of dozen people, and they expect the county to look after them. Can't be done when the sheriff of that county has only one, maybe two deputies, and's already got more ground than he can cover.

"Right now I'm in a worse fix than I've ever been. Got no deputies—one disappeared and the other'n's laid up. Got me really strapped. Hired a new man in Denver, but he can't be here for a while—and I'm needing somebody down there now.

"Folks are afraid there'll be more murders—and there's a good chance there will if we're dealing with some kind of a loony. What's more, the governor's raising Cain with me to do something about it—as if I'm not trying—and he's threatening to send in the militia, declare martial law, if I don't. Expect you can see what that'd do to my reputation as a lawman if he did that."

Foreman hadn't changed all that much after all, Lark decided. He was still looking out for John Foreman, planning, working toward some higher goal, which was probably all right and a good plan for any man to follow as long as he didn't step on a lot of others getting there. That hadn't been Foreman's way, however—at least not during the time he'd served in the army.

"Can't say as I blame the governor much—he dropped by my office this morning to talk things over. Told me the newspapers had gotten wind of the trouble down at Arabella and were starting to play it up. And some of the big muckety-mucks in his political party are riding him hard to get it all straightened out and hushed up. Expect I'd be pushing somebody to get it handled myself was I in his boots. A man's whole career can hang on something like this."

Foreman paused, took up his glass and downed the remainder of its contents. The men at the bar were talking among themselves, and somewhere else in the building a woman laughed. Still holding his empty glass, the lawman leaned back, cocked his head to one side and studied Prestridge.

"Job oughtn't to take you but a week, maybe ten days. I figure a man like you can clear it up that soon, but you'll draw a month's wages and expenses even if you wind it up in less time. The pay'll be fifty dollars plus another fifty dollars for expenses. That sound fair to you?"

A hundred dollars for a few days' work! It was a small fortune to a man who hadn't had a steady job in over two years.

"Sounds good to me."

"Then I take it you want the job?"

"Long as you understand I don't know anything about being a deputy."

"Not necessary in your case. It'll take a man with horse sense and plenty of guts to iron things out down there, and from serving with you in the army, I know you've got both."

"Then I reckon you've hired yourself a deputy."

"Fine," John Foreman said, pushing back his chair and coming to his feet. "Let's get over to my office. I'll write you out a letter of authority and dig you up a star, and you can be on your way."

4

"I expect it'll be a smart idea for you to go to Arabella just as you are, sort of, well, looking like a down-and-out saddle tramp," John Foreman said as he and Prestridge left the saloon and angled across the street for the lawman's office. "Meaning no offense, of course."

Lark nodded. "Whatever you say. Figure to outfit myself complete with some new duds when I get paid. What I'm wearing's seen its best days."

Foreman, making a point of speaking to every person encountered on the short journey, said: "Just hold off till you've got things cleared up down there, then come to me. I'll fix it with a friend of mine who's in the clothing business here to give you what might be called a lawman's discount on everything you need."

"Obliged," Prestridge said, but he had no thoughts of accepting any additional favors from John Foreman. Providing him with a well-paying job for which the lawman would get full value in return was one thing; allowing him to prevail upon an acquaintance to accommodate him was something else, and not his way.

"Here we are," Foreman said, turning into the doorway of his quarters. "This'll only take a few minutes."

Lark followed the lawman into the small, heat-filled room, furnished with desk, chair and several benches placed along the walls. All was neat and orderly and somehow reflected John Foreman's personality.

Two men were seated on one of the benches. One, a thin, dark, still-faced man in dusty black pants tucked inside stovepipe boots, a gray shield shirt, leather vest and flat-crowned hat, was a lawman. The star he wore bore the inscription DEPUTY U.S. MARSHAL.

Foreman gestured toward him as he sat down at his desk. "This here's Jess Cahoon, Lark. You can see what he is from his badge. Jess, this is Larkin Prestridge, the friend you heard me telling the governor about."

Cahoon nodded coolly. Foreman ducked his head at the second man. Tall, with sandy hair and small brown eyes, he was an apple-cheeked man with a friendly way.

"This gentleman's Ed Wheeler. From the Land Office," the lawman said.

Wheeler offered his hand smilingly, said, "A pleasure to meet you, Lark."

"Same here," Prestridge replied, and swung his attention about as he heard Foreman speak.

"Here's a deputy's star for you," the lawman said, extending the bit of metal to him. "I'll get that letter written now."

Prestridge dropped the star into a pocket. John

Foreman, taking pen and paper from a drawer in his desk, nodded approvingly.

"Good idea—keeping it quiet that you're a deputy until you've had the chance to look around. Some folks shut up tight when they find out they're talking to a lawman," he said, and fell to writing on an oblong of paper which bore some sort of official seal.

"When you aim to go down to Arabella?" Cahoon asked, wiping at the sweat on his forehead with a bandanna.

"Like for him to head out today," Foreman said before Lark could answer. "Things down there've been neglected for too long as it is—and you heard what the governor said."

"Yeh, I heard," Cahoon replied and shifted on the bench. The heat in the office was intense. "Asking quite a bit of Prestridge, ain't you, John?"

Foreman glanced up. "Meaning?"

"Hell, the man just rode in! Probably been in the saddle all day, from the looks of him—and you're wanting him to climb right back aboard his horse and light out on a two-day ride."

Lark grinned at the marshal, appreciating the man's interest in his welfare. It had been a long, hot day and he was not looking forward to extending it further. Jess Cahoon knew what it was to sit leather hour after hour—something John Foreman probably knew little about.

"Wouldn't think another night would make much difference," Wheeler observed, taking tobacco and papers from a pocket and starting to roll a cigarette.

Foreman stared thoughtfully into the street. "No, guess it wouldn't," he conceded. "Just that I'm anxious to get a man on the job down there." The lawman turned his attention to Prestridge. "I'll leave it up to you—ride out yet today or wait for morning. Either way'll be all right with me."

Prestridge said, "Fine," and let it drop, making no commitment as he continued to stand by while Foreman completed the letter he was writing.

When it was finished the lawman read it aloud, glanced about for approval, and receiving nods from Cahoon and Wheeler, folded the sheet. Locating an envelope in a drawer of the desk, he placed the letter inside and handed it to Lark.

"There anybody in Arabella you figure's all right to talk to?" he asked, thrusting the envelope inside his shirt.

"Can't answer that because I don't know," Foreman said frankly, and turned to the marshal. "You think of anybody he can depend on, Jess?"

Cahoon shook his head. "No, sure can't, but then I ain't much acquainted down there. How about you, Ed?"

Wheeler rubbed at his jaw. "Same goes for me."

"Just better plan on everybody being hostile and a possible suspect," Foreman said. "Then, after you've hung around a bit you'll be able to separate the sheep from the wolves—or I best say wolf—and know who you can trust. But don't take too long doing it. We've got to nail that murderer before he kills again."

"Going to take some good detective work," Cahoon said. "You ever done any of that, Prestridge?"

"Nope, out of my line. Told the sheriff that."

"He won't need to be a detective—I would've sent for a Pinkerton man if I thought that was what I ought to have," the sheriff said. "Common sense, that's what's called for down there—and I know Lark's got plenty of that."

"He better have a quick trigger finger, too," Ed Wheeler commented dryly.

"He's got that, too," the lawman stated confidently. And then to Lark, "Expect you could use a little advance on your wages."

Prestridge grinned. He had less than a dollar in his pockets. "Could for a fact."

Foreman again pulled open a drawer in his desk and procured a leather poke. Loosening the drawstrings, he obtained two double-eagles and handed them to Lark.

"Part of what you'll have coming," he said, returning the sack to its place. "Twenty dollars on your wages, and twenty for expenses. I'll give you the rest when the job's done. That agreeable?"

"Suits me fine," Prestridge said. He'd be able to treat the buckskin to a good feed of grain now and have a meal of steak with all the trimmings for himself.

"When you aiming to leave?" Foreman asked as Lark moved toward the door. "Up to you, of course, but I'd like to know."

"In the morning—first light," Prestridge said. "The marshal was right—it's been a long day, and a hot one. My horse is in no shape to go on without some rest, and the same goes for me. But don't fret about it—I'll be gone early."

"I won't worry about it—none of it, in fact," Foreman said. "Arabella's your problem now. I'm leaving it up to you to get it handled. Good luck."

"Obliged," Lark said, and nodding to Cahoon and Wheeler, stepped out onto the sidewalk.

"You leaving any special time, other'n first light?" Cahoon called from inside the office. "Expect to pull out myself about then. Could ride together if I knew by the clock when you're going."

Prestridge shook his head. He didn't want to be saddled with any set arrangements and thus be under obligation to leave at a specific time. It could be he'd take a notion to head out shortly after midnight, once the buckskin had rested and eaten and he'd cooled off himself; but on the other hand he might just hang around until daylight.

"Your company'd be appreciated, but you'd best not depend on me. Ain't exactly sure when I'll leave," he said, and continued on his way.

5

Lark Prestridge halted the buckskin, eyes on a half-dozen buzzards circling slowly above something in the valley beyond the hill rising before him. For several moments he watched the great, dark shadows as they prowled the sky, and then, raking the gelding with his spurs, he climbed to the crest of the rise.

Immediately he saw the object of the vultures' attention—a horse. A fine, healthy-looking animal, it lay a short distance down the slope, and riding to it, Lark saw that it had been shot—a single bullet in the head. Frowning, Prestridge glanced about. Farther on he could see a square, black scar where a field had been swept by fire. Another charred area, like the beginning of a vast checkerboard, was visible in the near distance.

This all probably had some connection with the mysterious murders in the area, Lark concluded, and swinging back to the summit of the hill, let his gaze take in the country for more signs of vandalism. He was unprepared for the breathtaking beauty that spread before him.

A lake was shimmering quietly on the floor of a broad valley, one fed by underground springs apparently, as there were no streams feeding into it. The grass along its flat beach was deep green, and the cottonwoods and other trees were full-blown and thick-trunked.

In the slanting afternoon sunlight he could count five houses—there were possibly six—from the ledge where he had halted the buckskin, and by looking closely could see hedgerows of rock and brush running down to the lake marking the land boundaries of the homesteaders.

The fields were lush, thriving with corn, melons and vegetables. Here and there were fruit trees, their limbs weighted and soon ready to be picked. A thought came to Lark Prestridge: were the owners of three of those fine farms the men who had been murdered? Or were there other homesteads elsewhere in the valley?

Nearby in a tangle of false sage and wild gooseberry a quail called plaintively. Lark turned his attention to the lonely sound, searched briefly with his eyes, and failing to locate the bird, raised his glance to a small gather of buildings two or three miles on beyond the lake. That would be the settlement of Arabella, he reckoned, and cutting the buckskin around, he moved off across the wooded slope in the direction of the town. As well get there, find a place to stay—and go to work.

It was eerily quiet. That fact struck Prestridge as he circled the lake with its enclosing homesteads. Except for the calling of the quail and an occasional burst of quacking from ducks on the water, nothing broke the tense, warm solitude.

Nor was there anyone in sight as he reached the end of Arabella's lone street and again drew to a halt while he had his first look.

Yankee Quale's Saloon, a low-roofed, paintless wooden structure, stood immediately to his right. Fifty yards farther on was the General Store of A. Hotchkiss. Across from it was another saloon, one much larger than the first. It was termed the Bullhead, and the neglected, nearly illegible letters on its high false front offered not only liquor but gambling, women, rooms for rent and meals. A short distance on from it was the Star Livery Stable & Blacksmith Shop, and next to it was the last business building on that side of the street, Doolittle's Feed & Seed Store.

A dozen or so tree-shaded residences, with yards covered by wild grass and bordered with flowers, made up the remainder of the settlement. Lying in a hollow, it was encircled by cedars, junipers, cottonwoods, sycamores and a varied assortment of sage, mahogany, rabbitbush and like shrubbery which lent a sort of separateness to the place as if it wanted nothing to do with the rest of the world.

Again Lark Prestridge was conscious of the ominous hush that prevailed. Foreman had not exaggerated when he said the town was panic-stricken; there was no sign of life anywhere, yet he knew people were present—in their homes, inside their business houses, all keeping under cover while they waited for the killer to strike again and wondering all the while just who that next victim would be.

Lark pulled off his battered hat, wiped its sweatband with a finger and swabbed his forehead with a sleeve. He'd make the Bullhead his quarters, he guessed, and smiled at the decision; he had no other choice—there was no alternative.

He'd ride on in, letting all who watched think him no more than a drifter, as John Foreman had suggested. Too, he'd need to go easy with his money and not make any show of it but give the impression he was near broke. That would be no big change; he'd been in that condition for so long he hardly knew otherwise.

He'd let it be known he was looking for work and aimed to hang around for a few days while he paid a call on all the homesteaders—and ranchers, if there were any close by—and see if there were any jobs to be had. That should keep anybody from becoming suspicious as to why he didn't move on.

And thinking of suspicion, he'd best suspect everybody he met of being the killer until he got a clear picture of who was who around Arabella. To put his trust in the wrong person just might cost him his life, and he wasn't ready to die yet—not after serving four years of war.

Replacing his hat, Lark roweled the buckskin gently and swung into the street. The clumps of grass growing there reflected the limited amount of traffic that moved along its brief length.

A range of mountains lay like a blue-gray haze some distance beyond the town, Lark now noticed, and as he pointed the gelding for the hitch rack in front of the Bullhead, he wondered what they were called. He was a stranger to the country but it appealed to him, and the thought was now lodging in his mind to forget Arizona, accept any offer of a permanent job John Foreman apparently intended to make, and start building a new life here.

He drew abreast Yankee Quale's Saloon. There

was a horse pulled up to the rack at its side, he saw; he guessed the place had at least one customer despite the fear that gripped the town. However, as he passed by the open doorway he could see no one inside.

At the general store it was different. An elderly man in shirtsleeves and bib apron was standing well back in the building, fully visible. Nearby a woman, her face a severe, pale oval, could also be seen. Both observed his passage with no show of expression.

There were faces, too, at the windows of several residences, Lark saw, as he swung the buckskin in toward the rack at the corner of the Bullhead. A pitcher pump with its complementing water trough was a few strides on beyond, and Prestridge now veered toward it. The gelding had gone most of the day without a drink and deserved a few swallows.

Pulling up to the trough, Lark slackened the reins, and remaining in the saddle, allowed the buckskin to lower his head and slake his thirst. On impulse Lark decided to dismount, ease the dull ache in his back and leg muscles. He'd been riding steadily since sunrise. Leaning forward, he started to swing down. In that fragment of time a gunshot shattered the hush blanketing the settlement. Prestridge reacted instinctively. Throwing himself into a low dive, he went full length to the ground.

6

Grim, angry, mouth filled with loose dust, Lark Prestridge jerked to one side, began to roll. The shot had come from the trees and brush beyond the saloon. Heaving for breath, he gained the corner of the Bullhead, sprang erect. With the building now between him and the point where he figured the bushwhacker had been hiding, he drew his pistol and circled the structure at a run.

Reaching the rear of the saloon, Lark halted, dropped to a crouch. The undergrowth on the back side of the narrow, alleylike strip was a dense, gray-green wall. Squinting to favor his eyes, he carefully probed along its length for a sign of the killer. He could determine nothing.

Abruptly he rose, spurted from the corner of the Bullhead and reached the brush. Plunging into it, he cut hard left and hurried on, heedless of the noisy crackling and thrashing his headlong passage evoked, hopeful of a glimpse of the bushwhacker, if nothing more. Nothing.

He looked toward the saloon, slowed, halted. He

was beyond the spot where he thought the marksman had been hiding. A moment later he knew he was right. The faint but sharp odor of burned gunpowder still hung in the hot air.

For a long minute Lark remained motionless, his breathing restrained as he listened and glanced about. Finally he shrugged. The would-be killer had gone, disappeared without a trace or a sound. Holstering his weapon, Prestridge cut back through the brush and returned to where his horse waited.

Reaching the animal, which had shied off a few paces at the sound of the shot, Lark let his gaze sweep the street. No one had come out into the open. Ordinarily the firing of a gun would have brought men—some curious, others anxious, perhaps—on the run. He could see no indication of any reaction. Pure fear had locked everyone inside.

Taking the buckskin's reins, Prestridge started for the hitch rack. He frowned, brushed at the dust and sweat on his face as, sudden excitement over, his mind resumed its normal functioning and reasoning, and presented a question. If it had been the mysterious killer who had fired at him, how did he know who he was? No one in Arabella was aware of his coming, or why. That the killer would go to such pains to ambush a stranger in the center of the town in broad daylight didn't make sense.

Word would have had to come from John Foreman's office—perhaps even Foreman himself, Lark thought wryly, recalling again the nature of the man. But such a possibility made no sense either. Foreman had gone to some lengths to impress upon him the importance of getting the killer, intimating that it all had a very strong and direct bearing on his career. No, regardless of past experiences with the man, and the fact that he held him in low regard, he doubted Foreman was any party to the attempt.

But there were undoubtedly others who knew that he was being dispatched to the settlement—or suspected as much—and since he had not ridden out until the following morning, a rider leaving that preceding evening would have had ample time to reach Arabella well ahead of him and warn the murderer. And if that were true, then the killer was not acting alone and some sort of conspiracy existed—likely someone close to Foreman.

That could include any number of people, starting with the territorial governor and extending on to Deputy Marshal Jess Cahoon, Land Office man Ed Wheeler, the patrons who had been in the Silver Star Saloon and various other friends they had encountered on the street.

Lark shrugged as he wrapped the buckskin's lines around the crossbar of the rack. Such a list would be lengthy—and very possibly would have no bearing on the incident at all. The bushwhacker—the killer—could be some sort of lunatic, as most thought, and could have simply taken it into his head to shoot down the first person he happened to see. Regardless, he'd best make the most of the incident, see what developed.

Pulling his rifle from its boot, he hung it in the crook of an arm and crossed to the entrance of the Bullhead. Pausing just outside, Lark pulled off his hat, dusted himself briefly while he had a final look around, and then entered.

The Bullhead appeared much larger than Arabella's needs might require—or it could be that, deserted, it seemed so. A main floor complete with bar, tables, chairs; a corner devoted to chuck-a-luck, faro and other games of chance; a small square, roped off, with piano where dancing could be enjoyed; and an adjoining room that supplied quarters for the restaurant. A balcony, across the rear wall of the large room and reached by a narrow stairway, indicated the second floor, where lay the rental quarters.

Three men were leaning against the bar as Lark stepped inside. All were facing him, and as he let his flat eyes meet theirs in subtle challenge, they turned away and resumed their drinks. The bartender, a lean, florid individual, dark hair thinning, waited woodenly for Prestridge to reach the counter and make known his desire.

"Whiskey," Lark said, laying the Henry on top of the counter and shaking his head wonderingly. "Mind telling me what the hell's going on around here?"

The bartender, setting a shot glass in front of Prestridge, filled it from a quart bottle and glanced up. "Meaning?"

"Meaning who took a shot at me—what else?" Lark said peevishly. "And why? Just rode in, fixing to get myself a drink and maybe stay over a night or two—and I damn near get killed? What's going on?"

The bartender slid a glance to his three customers. All were again considering Lark, this time with quiet speculation. One, a tall, flat-faced man with a gray spade beard and trailing mustache, stirred indifferently.

"He sure can't be the one, Phin," he said, eyes on the bartender. "Couldn't've took a shot at himself."

The bartender swore. "Hell, I know that! What

I said was maybe he was the one, when he first rode up—him being a stranger and all that."

Prestridge tossed off his drink, set the empty glass down and stared expectantly at the man behind the counter.

"I'm waiting, Phin—that your name?"

"Phin Gribble. This here's my place," the barman replied.

"Well, Phin, you aim to let me in on what's going on or am I going to spend the rest of my life trying to figure out what this is all about?"

Lark hooked his elbows on the edge of the bar, let his glance move from Gribble to the customers and back again. A hard smile cracked his lips and he hoped he was putting over the idea that he was no more than a drifter, passing through, and indignant at being caught up in something of which he had no understanding.

The spade-bearded man stirred. "Where you from, friend?"

Lark shook his head. "Don't usually consider that anybody's business," he said, "but this being a sort of special occasion—me getting shot at—I reckon I'll make an exception. Come up from Texas way."

Over in the archway leading into the restaurant an elderly woman, apron draped across her front, features a beefy red, hair imprisoned in a net, stepped into view.

"You want me cooking up any more'n I did yesterday?" she called, looking at Phin.

Gribble glanced at Prestridge. "You staying the night?"

Lark raised his eyes to the open doorway as if gauging the sun. "Getting on to dark. Might as well."

"We've got one customer," Phin said to the woman. "Fix up about the same."

The cook turned, disappeared into the restaurant. Quiet again filled the saloon. Lark rattled his empty glass on the counter and shoved it toward the bottle of whiskey.

"Can use another—that bullet came a mite close," he said, and then added: "You ain't said yet what's going on here. It some kind of a secret?"

Gribble smiled wanly. "Nope, it ain't. We're just all a bit surprised that you don't know."

Lark's shoulders lifted, fell. "Stranger. First time I've been through here."

"Well, we've got us a crazy killer running loose," Gribble said. "Done killed five men. You danged near turned out to be number six."

7

Prestridge stared at Phin Gribble for a long breath, feigning surprise. Then, frowning, he said: "Five men?"

The saloon owner bobbed. "Five—"

"And you don't know who's doing it—no ideas at all?"

"No, we sure don't," the tall man with the spade beard said. "We figure he's a loony of some kind—mad at everybody for some reason."

"Most folks think he's some jasper that worked around here and maybe got fired, or run off a job, and now he's taking his peeve out on the whole country around here." It was another of the customers at the bar speaking. "Makes sense to me."

"Could be it, all right," Lark agreed, working at laying a solid footing. "What's the law doing about it?"

"Ain't got none here—no town marshal, I mean," Gribble replied. "Sheriff from up at Kingdom City—that's the county seat—sent a couple of deputies. One of them got cold feet and took off soon as he seen what he was up against. Other'n got hisself throwed off his horse. Accident, he claimed."

"Weren't no accident," the tall man said flatly. "Was something caused that horse to throw him—and I'm laying odds that something was the killer."

Lark toyed with his glass of whiskey, finally downed it. So far he'd learned nothing more than John Foreman had already told him, but he felt it was necessary to play along, give the impression that he was a stranger just riding through.

"Sure seems like somebody would've got a look at that killer," he said doubtfully. "Man just can't disappear—like he was smoke. He use a gun?"

"Rifle—from off in the brush like he tried on you," the saloonman said.

Prestridge grinned wryly. "Got to admit I didn't see nothing—or find any sign when I had a look at where he was standing. Who'd he shoot?"

"Homesteaders. One by the name of Gunderson—Al Gunderson. Another was Tom Lockwood and the third was Levi Trent."

"You said he killed five."

"All told. Three of them was homesteaders. Other two were hired hands—Charley White and Ben Wilson."

"They all down there along that lake I saw as I rode in?"

"Yeh, Arabella Lake—same name as the town. There's homesteads all around it, like spokes in a wheel. Couple of them empty now—Minton's place and Levi Trent's. Trent's one of them that got killed, Minton pulled out—same as some of the others are about to do."

"Had a hunch there maybe was something going on down there," Lark said. "Saw a couple of fields that'd been burnt over—and the buzzards were after a horse that had been shot."

"Them fires were more'n a week ago. Ain't nobody got any idea what started them. The horse I ain't heard about," Phin said.

"Happened probably yesterday morning," Lark said.

His anger at being shot at had long since cooled as he continued to dig and pry for information. He was taking no pleasure from the means he was employing to obtain such, however; a voice within him was decrying his dishonesty.

"You all could be right—thinking it's some bird with a big grudge," he continued. "But on the other hand it's maybe somebody wanting the land and water."

"Who'd want it—except another homesteader?"

At Phin's question Prestridge shrugged. "There any ranches around? Always needing more range or water, seems."

"Some fine places to the north of here," spade beard said. "Biggest one's Reuben Cade's Lazy C outfit."

"He pushed for more land?"

"Not so's you'd notice. Reuben's got close to a hundred thousand acres of good grass—and he sure ain't got no need for water, now or ever before. Coyote Creek runs clean across his range, same as it does the other ranches. Stream heads up in the mountains above them, runs good the year around."

"Don't sound like any ranchers are behind it," Lark admitted. He was beginning to take some stock in the possibility that it was a kill-crazy maniac who had committed the murders, but it was still too early to make up his mind. "Sure is a puzzlement."

"Can say that again," spade beard said, and pulled back from the bar. "Reckon I best be getting along, Phin," he said to the bartender while nodding to Prestridge. "You keep your eyes peeled!"

"Same to you, Amos," Gribble said as the tall man, followed by the two with him, moved off for the door in the back of the saloon.

When they had gone Lark said, "He a homesteader around here?"

"Amos?" Phin said, removing the used glasses from the bar. "Nope—he's got a ranch west of here. Not much of a place—just enough to keep him and them two that was with him eating regular. That's the way he wants it. Could do better if he was of a mind to."

"Some folks are like that, all right. Makes for easy living. What's the rest of his name?"

"Scarborough. Amos Scarborough."

Prestridge tapped on his glass, called for another drink. "Who're them two with him?"

Phin Gribble gave Lark a swift, appraising glance, took up the bottle of whiskey and poured. "Relatives of his he sort of looks after. Both a mite backward. Amos takes care of them like they was his young'uns."

The door in the rear of the saloon opened again and the elderly man Lark had seen standing, with a woman, inside the general store appeared. White bib apron folded across his waist, he hurried to the end of the bar and halted. Phin moved to that part of the counter, poured him a drink from a bottle apparently being kept separate. The man gulped it down, and nodding to the bartender as well as

Lark, turned on a heel and hastily departed by the same route that he'd come.

"Andy Hotchkiss," Gribble said in reply to the questioning look on Prestridge's face. "Owns the general mercantile store."

Lark nodded. "Recollect seeing him there when I rode by. Everybody around here as scared as he seems to be?"

"Just about—only that ain't the main reason he acts the way he does. Wife of his is dead set against drinking and he has to sneak over whenever he wants a nip, get it on the sly."

Lark grinned. "Something wrong with her nose? You'd think she'd smell it on his breath."

Gribble leaned forward, peered through a dust-filmed window of his establishment. "Andy's plenty careful," he said, and pointed.

Prestridge came about, followed the saloonman's leveled finger. Hotchkiss had produced a large cigar, was puffing at it vigorously as he crossed the street to his store.

"But you talking about folks being scared," Gribble said. "They are for sure. Business has come to a flat stop. Ain't nobody doing nothing, hardly. The people living out on the flats and in the valleys around here, that used to do their trading here in Arabella, do their buying up in Crawfordsville now. We got only local trade—and there ain't enough of it to keep a jackrabbit alive.

"Place of mine was always pretty busy this time of day—not a lot of customers, understand, unless it was a weekend or some holiday. I could always figure on having five or six standing at the bar, another half a dozen gambling or fooling around with the girls.

"Now you don't see nobody—not even at night

when things was always good. The girls working here pulled out, too scared to stay around—wasn't no money to be made anyway since there wasn't no customers. Amos and his two cousins and you are the only people that've come in today—not counting Andy Hotchkiss, that being his own bottle. Might be a couple of cowhands drop by tonight, but there ain't nothing for sure about it."

Gribble paused, rubbed disconsolately at the worn surface of his counter with a moist rag. "Best I tell you—"

"Name's Lark Prestridge."

"Best I tell you, Prestridge, you're the only guest I got for my rooms, and you'll be the only one eating supper in my restaurant, save me. Want you to know that in case you're inclined to be a mite spooky—and I won't fault you none after that killer making you eat dust—"

Lark reached into a pocket for a silver dollar with which to pay for his drinks, shrugged. "Expect if I was showing good sense I'd keep riding," he said, "but I don't much appreciate getting shot at. Sort of riles me."

Gribble picked up the silver coin, dropped it into a box and returned a lone dime change to Lark.

"Know how you feel," he said. "Been some of the folks around here up and pull out on account of that killer. Just loaded up what they had and took off. Got to admit I done a bit of thinking along that line myself—then I figured, what the hell's the use? No matter where I'd go and settle like as not trouble would turn up—and a man can't keep on running all his life."

"Exactly how I feel about it," Lark said. "Running never solved anything. . . . There a barn out back where I can stable my horse?"

"Sure. I'll look after him, if you want."

"Be obliged. Now which room—"

"Can have your choosings. Just climb them steps, and take whichever one suits your fancy. Like I said, you're the only renter on the place."

Lark nodded, took up his rifle and started for the door. "Need to get my saddlebags and blanket roll."

"I'll fetch them after I've put your horse in a stall," Gribble said accommodatingly. "You go on ahead, pick yourself a room. Can figure to come down to supper in about an hour. I'll bring you up a bucket of fresh water so's you can wash up, when I come with your gear."

Prestridge smiled, reversed his direction and moved toward the stairway. As a cash customer he certainly was getting the royal treatment.

◎ 8 ◎

The room Lark Prestridge chose was near the end of the hallway that divided the second floor of the Bullhead and offered a window that allowed him to look down on the street as well as most of the town. There was some advantage to be had in that, he believed.

The room was small and apparently had been closed for some length of time; it was stuffy and filled with stale, heated air. A ragged, faded rug was centered on the floor, and yellowing paper, coming loose in several places, covered the walls. A bed with a crackling cornhusk mattress, a scarred rocking chair, a chiffonier with drawers that stuck, and a wash stand with pitcher, bowl and mirror completed the furnishings.

But it was a change from sleeping on the trail or in the back room of a saloon, and Lark had no complaints. He had managed to open the window, allowing the trapped air to escape and the evening's coolness to seep in, when a rap on the door sounded and the panel swung inward. Phin Gribble, a bucket of water in one hand, Lark's saddlebags hung over a shoulder and blanket roll in the other hand, entered.

Tossing the latter onto the bed, he filled the china pitcher from the bucket and, coming about, nodded to Prestridge.

"Your horse has been took care of, and I expect this fixes you up," he said and then as if remembering, crossed to the lamp bracketed on a wall and visibly measured the oil in its reservoir. "Like as not that'll hold you for tonight, but if you need more, just help yourself to any of the lamps in the other rooms."

"Don't expect to be using it much," Lark said. "Been a long day. Aim to turn in soon's I get a bite to eat."

"Supper'll be ready time you come down," Phin said and moved toward the door. "Going to have some company after all," he added, pausing. "Four cowhands on their way to Crawfordsville, just rode in. They figure to eat and do a bit of drinking before they go on."

"You know them?" Prestridge asked, beginning to strip off his shirt.

"Nope, all strangers," the saloonman replied, studying Lark narrowly. "Why?"

"Was just wondering. Them stopping over means they don't know about the killings."

"Guess not," Phin said, shrugging, "or else they plain don't give a damn. See you downstairs."

Gribble resumed his departure, stepping out into the now dark hallway and pulling the door closed behind him. Lark continued to undress, pausing once to cross over and turn the key in the lock to secure the panel, after which he filled the bowl from the pitcher, washed himself down and then shaved.

He had no change of clothing other than a clean shirt, drawers and fresh socks, and deciding that making use of them would in no way destroy his pretense of being a penniless drifter, he put them on. After that he shook the dust from his pants, wiped off his worn boots, and thus having done all he could to improve his appearance, found himself ready.

Strapping on his pistol and hanging the Henry rifle in the crook of his left arm, Lark descended to the lower floor. It was now full dark outside, and Gribble had lit the chandeliers in the saloon just as if the usual run of business was expected.

And there was an increase that Lark knew the saloonman had not anticipated. As he cut his way through the tables for the restaurant, Prestridge noted not only the cowhands Phin had mentioned, but a fairly well-dressed woman accompanied by a man in a business suit, and two sun-darkened individuals, probably father and son from the similarity, wearing coarse shirts, heavy shoes and bib overalls—homesteaders, no doubt, or hired hands working for such.

Lark wondered what had brought about the increase in patrons as he reached the restaurant, entered and settled down at a table placed against the wall—well away from the windows facing the street. Likely the man and woman, probably a drummer and his wife or lady friend, were just passing through, as were the cowhands, and knew nothing of Arabella's problem. But the two homesteaders—

Lark's thoughts were interrupted by the arrival of the waitress, who proved to be the elderly, heavy-set woman he'd seen earlier and who also served as the cook.

"Supper's fried meat and potatoes, butter beans, greens, hot biscuits and honey, coffee," she said, and then continued: "If that ain't suiting you, I can fry you up some bacon and eggs."

"Regular supper sounds good," Prestridge said. "Can use that coffee now."

The woman turned and headed for a door in the back of the room, one that evidently led into the kitchen. Midway she paused, looked toward the arched entrance to the saloon area. The drummer and his companion were entering, moving to a table in a corner and settling down. Elsewhere in the Bullhead the sounds of laughter, shouts and deep-toned conversations had brought the place alive, but outside Arabella continued to lie in deep silence.

It was pleasant there in the dimly lit room, and Lark, despite the situation he faced, was enjoying himself. Months had passed since he'd been in a position to buy a good, complete meal, and the prospect of that and of sleeping in a bed under a roof was going to be a welcome change. It would be fine if someday he could afford such luxuries more often, and maybe—just maybe—if things went right for him this time and he ended up with a permanent job, he could. But that called for his finding the murderer who was running loose in Arabella before he killed again, and so far, he had to admit, he'd made little if any progress.

His food came, a large platter covered with meat, browned potatoes and other well-cooked, tasty items. The biscuits were large, light as thistledown, and the coffee, brought only now and not earlier as he'd requested, was strong and black.

He fell to with relish, only vaguely aware of the noise in the saloon and the quiet conversing of the drummer and his woman on the adjacent side of the room. Lark ate leisurely, treated himself to a third cup of coffee, and then, finally satisfied, rose to go. As he laid money for the check the heavy-set waitress had left on his table, he heard bootheeled steps, and glancing up, saw the quartette of cowhands entering. All had been drinking, were now jovial, broadly smiling men in the best of humor.

They selected a table at the window, he noted as he moved on and bent his own steps toward the bar, where he could see Phin Gribble at his post. A drink would set well now, then he'd head for his room and stretch out on the bed for a night's good sleep.

"Everything suit you, Lark?" the saloonman greeted as Prestridge bellied up to the bar.

"Fine," Lark replied. "Was the best meal I've had in a long time."

Gribble bobbed, grinned, well pleased. "Glad to hear it. I'll tell Nellie. You wanting something?"

"Shot of whiskey," Prestridge said. "Anything happening?"

"You mean about that killer? No, nothing, leastwise not so far this evening."

Lark glanced around. The two homesteaders were at one table, and three other men who had arrived after he'd gone in for supper were playing cards at another.

"Business seems to've picked up plenty for you."

"Yeh, folks've kind've forgot about the killings, I reckon, since you got here."

Lark stiffened. Had he, despite his care, tipped his hand? "What's that mean?"

"That you've kind of changed things some—that

bushwhacker missing you this afternoon like he did. Guess it made folks realize he's only a man after all and not some kind of a devil that can't nobody beat."

"Wrong thing for them to think," Prestridge said. "I was plain lucky. They go getting careless it could cost them their lives. Everybody here live in Arabella or nearby?"

"Well, no—only Linus Ford and his boy, Frank, them two homesteaders over there. They've got a place along the lake. Them cowhands and that fellow and his woman are passing through."

"How about the cardplayers?"

"All from south of here. Drop in now and then."

"How far south?"

"About twenty mile. Come up just to get their snouts off the grindstone a bit," Phin said, pouring Lark a drink. "You riding on in the morning?"

Prestridge downed his liquor, paused to listen to a burst of laughter coming from the restaurant. The cowhands were continuing to enjoy themselves.

"I've not made up my mind yet," he said. "May just hang around for a few days. That cook of yours is putting out the best bait of grub I've run into in a long time."

"So you told me," the saloonman said quietly, again eyeing Lark thoughtfully, cagily. "There anything special I can do for you?"

It was Prestridge's turn to wonder. He considered Gribble with equal circumspection. Something in the barman's tone told him that his identity was no longer a secret, that Phin somehow knew, or perhaps suspected, why he was in Arabella. But he was not ready to admit it yet—not on the possibility that Gribble was only guessing.

Abruptly he picked up his rifle and pulled back from the counter.

"I'll be turning in. Been a hard day. G'night."

"Good night," Gribble responded as Prestridge moved toward the stairway.

Reaching the first of the steps Lark, suddenly aware of weariness, began a slow ascent. Gaining the top, he hesitated, eyes reaching down the length of the corridor that led to his room. There were no lamps, and the darkness of the narrow hallway was relieved only by faint streaks of light filtering through the dusty panes of the window set high in the wall facing the street.

The sounds of laughter coming from the restaurant below again reached him as he started to continue. He took one full step, halted, a wariness claiming him. A dark shape was crouched in the shadows at the end of the hall.

9

Lark Prestridge let the rifle slip forward in his hand until he felt the hammer under his thumb and his forefinger on the trigger. Squinting, he studied the bent shape, unable to tell for certain if it was a man or simply some object—trash, a piece of furniture previously unnoticed by him that had been placed there. Such was a logical explanation; his door, like that of the room opposite, was five or six feet from the corridor's end, and the area created was ideal for—

The blur in the darkness moved. Prestridge lunged to one side as the glint of metal in the weak light caught his eye. He fired the Henry from the hip, the blast of the rifle overriding that of the pistol shot coming from the opposite end of the hall. He heard the dull thud of a bullet as it buried itself in the ceiling above him, heard also the startled yells arising below. Powder smoke hung about him, filling the confined area with its pungent odor. Lark waited, having already levered a fresh cartridge into the chamber of his weapon—

a procedure done automatically and without conscious thought instantly after pressing the trigger.

There was no further movement in the shadows below the window. Slowly, rifle still hanging loose and ready in his arms, and with the quick hammer of boots on the steps breaking the hush, Lark started down the corridor. A tautness gripped him as he realized what it meant; a second attempt had been made to kill him, thus proving the first try was no accident, no mistake.

"What's all the shooting?"

Lamplight flooded the hallway as Phin Gribble's voice registered on him. He did not turn, but continued on, still wary and not fully convinced the figure stretched out on the floor was dead. He could hear others with the saloonkeeper, guess that about everyone he'd seen downstairs, with the possible exception of the drummer's woman and the cook, had come rushing up to see what had happened.

Lark reached the prostrate, face-down figure. Both arms were outflung, the right hand still grasping a pistol. Prestridge kicked the weapon clear of the man's nerveless fingers, and then, squatting, felt for a pulse. There was none, and rolling the dead man over, Lark drew himself upright and stepped back. The dark, square-jawed face with its stubble of beard was unfamiliar to him. At that moment he heard Gribble whistle softly in surprise.

"You know him?" he asked, turning to the barman.

Phin, holding the lamp above his head, nodded. "Name's Gabe Hartline. Sort of a hard case."

The other men were crowding in close for a

better look, some murmuring, others remaining quiet.

"He from around here?" Lark asked.

Again the saloonkeeper nodded. "Works for Reuben Cade—the Lazy C. Cowpuncher."

Prestridge gave that thought. Cade, the cattleman. The Lazy C ranch. One of the nearby spreads —the largest, he believed someone had said, and in no need of either land or water.

"You figure he's the same one that took a potshot at you when you rode in?"

It was the older of the two homesteaders—Ford, Gribble had said their names were. He was a squat, dirt-stained man with a ragged yellow beard.

Prestridge's shoulders stirred. "Expect he is."

There was a long silence, broken finally by the younger Ford. "You—you reckon he's the killer that's been running loose around here?" he said in a hopeful voice.

Again there was hush, ended this time by Phin Gribble. "Who knows? He sure could be, but it's kind of hard to figure that Gabe'd be him. What reason would he have for murdering them fellows?"

"Didn't need no reason!" the elder Ford stated flatly. "Was crazy, plumb crazy!"

"Them kind just ups and shoots anybody that's handy," the younger Ford added.

Which could be considered true, Prestridge thought, only it wasn't that way where he and Hartline were concerned. The man had lain in ambush for him on the street, and failing, had then entered the Bullhead, probably by a rear door so as to pass unseen, and again waited for him. That was not the way of a crazed impulse killer; this indicated planning.

But it still made no sense. Why would Hartline

set out to kill him? Make two tries at it, in fact, assuming the Lazy C cowhand was the one who had fired that shot from the brush at him—and Lark felt certain he was. But why?

"I'm betting he's the killer," the older Ford was saying. He and Phin had apparently been explaining to the strangers what it was all about. "Be like him to try and kill this here fellow."

"Why, if he's a stranger?" one of the cowhands protested. "Don't make no sense."

"That's just it—it don't need to," the homesteader replied.

The rider's friends, sobered as was he by the sight of the dead man, continued to stare at Hartline's lifeless body. Finally one shrugged.

"Well, howsomever you figure it, killer or not, that child ain't going to be shooting nobody now—not in the shape he's in."

That broke the sobriety of his companions, and all laughed. The man who had first voiced a doubting question rubbed at his jaw.

"No, sir, not less he's aiming to pick a fight with the devil," he said. "Come on, let's go finish our eating. I want to get back in that saloon and do a little serious drinking before we head for home."

The riders swung about, tramped the short distance to the head of the stairs and began a noisy descent, the thud of their heels echoing hollowly in the quiet building.

Phin Gribble had set the lamp on the floor, was studying Hartline's slack features. He glanced up at Lark.

"Just could be Gabe's the one that's been doing all the killing around here. Always been sort of odd—keeping to himself and the like. You reckon he is the murderer?"

Prestridge, leaning against the wall, shrugged. "Being a stranger, I wouldn't have no opinion. I'm damn sure of one thing, however; he tried to kill me—and I expect he's the one who took a shot at me earlier. I'm trying to puzzle out why."

"You aim to look into it?"

"Bet on it! Not about to let somebody get away with that."

A knowing smile pulled at Phin Gribble's lips as if he had just come to a satisfactory conclusion. The older Ford clawed at his beard.

"Man there's stone dead. You ain't going to get nothing out of him. So where'll you start?"

Lark considered the homesteader in the yellow glow of the lamp. Ford was plenty curious for a bystander; also, with the killer roaming free he and his son had been out and around, seemingly unafraid of becoming victims of the murderer. Could there be some connection between Ford and his son, and the killer?

Prestridge broke off the thought, set it aside in his mind. Suspecting the Fords, who were in the same precarious situation as all the other homesteaders living around Arabella Lake, struck him as ridiculous. But at this point he was discarding no possibility, not the remotest, until he could be certain.

"I'll start by toting this Hartline out to the Lazy C ranch," Prestridge said. "Maybe Reuben Cade can tell me why a man working for him wanted to kill me."

The younger Ford wagged his head. "I'm still saying he's the crazy killer—"

"He sure could be," Phin said, neither agreeing or disagreeing. "What'll we do with him now, Lark?"

The drummer, who had stood by silently during the conversation, said, "He ought to be taken to the undertaker for burying."

"We ain't got one," Gribble said. "Anyways, Prestridge there's hauling him out to the Lazy C ranch. They can plant him."

"You want us to put him in the barn?" the elder Ford asked. "Me'n my boy are leaving—can carry him down as we go."

"I'd be obliged to you," Lark said. "Probably left his horse out back."

"Expect he did," Ford said and, motioning to his son, moved toward the body.

"Take him down the back stairs, Linus," Gribble said, picking up the lamp. "I'll hold the door open for you."

The saloonkeeper hurried along the hallway as the two homesteaders, one taking Hartline by the legs, the other, the shoulders, lifted the body easily, and quickly followed. Lark, the drummer beside him, trailed more slowly, Prestridge halting when he reached the landing at the top of the stairs. The drummer started to descend, hesitated, glance on Gribble now returning.

"Guess I'll never get used to how easy folks take death out in this country. Seems—well—indecent."

Lark considered the man thoughtfully. "You in the war?"

"No."

"That was pretty indecent, too," he said dryly, and turned to face Gribble. The drummer made some sort of reply, but Lark let it pass unheard, and the man went on down the stairs.

Phin smiled, halted. "Except you're needing a drink after all that," he said. Down below the cowhands were noisily finishing their interrupted supper in the restaurant and the drummer had rejoined his lady friend at a table near the bar.

Prestridge said, "Nope, sleep's what I need. Like to ask something, however."

"Yeh?"

"Those two homesteaders—the Fords. Their place is over on the lake, you said. Seems a mite unusual they'd be out running around at night with that killer loose."

Gribble gave that thought, nodded. "Yeh, comes down to it—it is. Don't recollect ever seeing either Linus or Frank—or the other son, Earl—around here at night before—leastwise not in a long time. Why're you asking?"

Lark turned away. "Was just curious."

Gribble laid his hand on Prestridge's arm. "You ain't thinking maybe they're back of the killings—"

Lark waved the man to silence, pulled away. "Now, that wouldn't make any sense, would it?" he said, avoiding a direct answer. "Only trying to get everything straight in my head. . . . See you in the morning."

10

The buildings of Cade's Lazy C ranch lay in a broad, green hollow of the low hills. On below a short distance, Prestridge could see a small pond glistening in the early-morning sunlight. A narrow ditch angling down from the rancher's upper range, where it apparently branched off Coyote Creek, was its source of supply. A windmill rising sturdily in the yard behind the main house, however, provided water for the household.

There were many trees about, and the well-kept structures, reflecting prosperity, had garden plots not only of vegetables, but of varied and brightly colored flowers as well. Lark had noted no stock as he came from the settlement trailing the horse that carried Gabe Hartline's body, but now he could see Cade's herd, split into many small jags, grazing on the distant slopes and flats and in the shallow valleys.

Reuben Cade was well off—probably wealthy, Lark reckoned as he rode down a gentle grade for the gate marking the entrance to the ranch proper.

It was hardly possible that a man in his position could in any way be connected with the attempts on his life, Prestridge felt, but the fact that Hartline worked for Cade made him party to it.

Prestridge saw Cade, or assumed it was the rancher, on the porch fronting the main house as he drew up to the hitch rack. A young woman was with him, and together they were sitting at a small table having coffee. On beyond the house, across the hardpack that separated it from the crew's quarters, he noticed several Lazy C riders. Eyes on him and the horse he was leading, they began to move forward.

Features stiff, anger again stirring through him, Lark nodded coldly to the rancher. "You Reuben Cade?"

Cade, a large man, dark hair thinning, thick mustache laced with gray, returned Prestridge's consideration with matching coolness. The girl, also dark-haired, with quiet blue eyes and a firm set to her lips, was probably the rancher's daughter, Lark reasoned; she was much too young to be his wife.

"That's me," Cade replied gruffly. "Who've you got there?"

"It's Gabe Hartline, Mr. Cade," one of the punchers said from the corner of the house. Abruptly pulling his pistol, he moved toward Lark. Two other men nearby immediately stepped in behind him.

Prestridge considered them coldly, hand resting on his own weapon. "Back off," he warned softly.

Reuben Cade came to his feet. "Let it go, boys," he said, waving them back. "I'll handle it."

The cowhands halted, faces stiff, angry. "He was a Lazy C puncher—" one began.

"Said I'd handle it, Tom!" the rancher snapped and put his attention on Lark. "Now, who're you?"

"Name's Prestridge. Understand Hartline works for you."

The rancher glanced at the cowhands, at the girl who had risen and was now standing beside him. Trim, she was most attractive.

"No, he don't," Cade said.

The girl flung him a quick, puzzled look that was not missed by Prestridge. The three cowhands stirred uncertainly.

"Was told in town that he did."

"I ain't caring a damn what you've been told," the rancher stated flatly. "He's not working for me."

Lark, studying the man, gave the words thought. "What you're saying is that he's not working for you now. How about yesterday?"

Cade half-turned, picked up his cup of coffee and took a swallow. Except for the creaking of the windmill turning lazily in the slight breeze, there was complete silence.

"You calling me a liar in a roundabout way?"

Lark shifted on his saddle, shrugged. "Seems you're telling me a lie in a roundabout way."

Cade's shoulders stiffened. A faint smile parted the girl's lips. Prestridge waited out a long minute, continued.

"Hartline tried to kill me last night in the Bullhead saloon. Hid out in the dark. I figure he was the one who tried to bushwhack me earlier—when I rode in. I'm looking for the reason why."

Reuben Cade set the cup back on the table. "And you think I can give it to you. Well, I can't. Maybe Hartline did ride for me—once—and maybe he didn't, but I sure never put him up to shooting you. Why would I? Never seen you before in my life."

"The why of it's just why I'm here," Lark said coolly, extending the reins of the dead man's horse toward the riders collected at the corner of the house. The one called Tom came forward slowly and accepted the leathers, all the while looking questioningly at Cade. The rancher nodded his permission.

"Take him down to the barn—and a couple of you nail a coffin together. Can bury him out there on the hill," he said, and swung back to Lark. "Step down, Prestridge, have a cup of coffee with me—and my daughter. Can talk this thing over."

There was no warmth in the rancher's invitation, only a businesslike offer to get a problem settled. Lark hardly noticed the condescension; he'd been right about the girl—she was Cade's daughter, and that verification pleased him.

Coming off the buckskin, he wound the reins around the crossbar of the rack and stepped up onto the porch.

"My daughter, Martha," the rancher said, gesturing at the girl. "Don't recollect your saying your full name."

"Lark Prestridge."

Martha nodded her acknowledgment, and Cade, motioning Lark to a chair, sat down. There were several more cups on the table alongside the large pot of coffee, and taking one of those, Martha Cade filled it and placed it before Prestridge. Apparently the rancher held court for his hired help on the porch each morning, at which time he gave instructions for the day and heard complaints. Lark guessed he'd arrived not long after this particular day's session was over.

"You're a stranger around here," the girl said, refilling her father's cup. She had resumed her place at the table, and her quiet graciousness did much to relieve the surly incivility of her father and lessen the tension. "Are you moving into our valley?"

Lark smiled at the girl, again felt a stir within him as she met his glance. "No, ma'am. Just passing through, mostly."

Reuben Cade's thick brows lifted. "Mostly?"

Prestridge shrugged. It was a fool thing to say. "Meaning, I'd stopped over for the night when this Hartline tried to gun me down. Stayed over to find out why."

The rancher grunted. Martha, her own cup filled, said, "Has it occurred to you that he may have mistaken you for someone else?"

Again the rancher's hostile features registered interest. Lark gave the suggestion consideration. "No, but I guess it's possible. He had a good look at me first time he tried, however. Was still daylight. Couldn't have made a mistake then."

"Unless he'd never seen you before and was going on a description somebody had given him."

"Somebody?"

"Yeh, somebody that might've hired Gabe to kill you," Reuben Cade said, nodding. "Girl, just maybe've you've got something there. Gabe Hartline rode fence for me and done some cowpunching, but he was a gunslinger, too—a hired gun. I know that for a fact."

"Could be it—but who'd want me dead?"

"Reckon you can answer that best, friend. You got some enemies hating your insides bad enough to want to see you in the graveyard? Or—maybe it's the law that's put a price on your head and the bounty hunters—"

"Nothing like that," Lark cut in. "Law's not wanting me, and far as enemies go I've got a few, same as any man, but I can't think of any hating me enough to pay for having me killed."

"That's something no man can be dead sure of," Cade said indifferently.

"It was probably a mistake on Hartline's part," Martha said, ignoring her parent's words. "He simply took you for someone else."

It was possible, Lark had to agree, but there were still shreds of doubt in his mind. "Could be the answer," he said, and then turned to Cade. "Some of the folks in town think maybe he was the killer that's been running loose around there. You figure there's a chance of that?"

Reuben Cade looked out over the grassy hills extending off to the south. The windmill still creaked slowly, and off where the garden lay warm and thriving in the sun a meadowlark whistled cheerily.

"Just could be," he said, "and again maybe not. What give them the idea?"

"Can't say exactly, excepting him making that try at shooting me."

"You ain't one of them sodbusters over around the lake, why'd he pick you? That don't make sense."

"If he was loco like folks seem to think he was, it don't have to," Lark said quietly. "Man that's gone over the edge for some reason never makes any sense in what he does—just strikes out at the first fellow handy. Saw a lot of that during the war."

"Those poor people," Martha murmured. "It

must be terrible for them—wondering who might be next."

"If there is a next," Cade said, rising. "Who knows—Gabe might've been the killer and there won't be no more murders. . . . I've got to get down to the south range."

"Papa," Martha said, laying her hand on his wrist, halting him. "We're short of help—and with Gabe Hartline gone now—I was wondering if you—if it wouldn't be a good idea to hire on Mr. Prestridge. Expect he's looking for a job."

"That so?" the rancher asked, glancing sharply at Lark.

Prestridge had come to his feet. He smiled at the girl. It was best he continue the role of drifter, although deceiving Martha went against the grain.

"Am sort of looking around—"

"Good. I'll keep you in mind," Cade said, and nodding curtly, stepped down off the porch and started briskly for the corrals on the far side of the hardpack.

The girl flushed slightly, managed a smile. "I'll see that he remembers," she said apologetically. "More coffee?"

Prestridge shook his head. "Obliged, but I'd best be getting back to town," he said, and hat in hand, moved toward his horse. "Was a pleasure meeting you. So long."

"Goodbye—"

11

As he rode through the gate, Prestridge turned, looked back. Martha raised her hand, waved. He touched the brim of his hat in response, and filled with a strange lightness, almost an elation, swung onto the road that led to Arabella.

Hartline . . . Lark's thoughts settled on the man. He was a hired gun, according to Reuben Cade, who worked only occasionally, and apparently just recently, for the Lazy C. He'd remember to ask Phin Gribble for verification of that.

Prestridge was still on the fence where the possibility of the gunman being the murderer was concerned. It could be, although he had to admit the idea advanced by the Cades—by Martha, actually—that Gabe Hartline had mistaken him for someone else was logical. But he wasn't fully convinced of that, either.

One thing, however, the thought that lurked in the back of his mind that Reuben Cade was in some way connected with the killings—one further strengthened when he'd learned that Hartline was one of Cade's hired hands—appeared improbable now. There simply was no reason for the rancher to be involved. He possessed all the land and water he could use, had reached the point in life where he need only to sit back and reap the benefits of previous years' labor; why would he covet any of the homesteads at Arabella Lake?

The fact that Hartline worked for him should be considered only incidental. It could be that he'd taken a job on the Lazy C so as to not arouse suspicion while he awaited the chance to kill the man—whoever he was—that had brought him there.

But that assumed what Martha Cade had suggested was a fact; Hartline had been hired to kill someone that he resembled. What if that was in no way true? What if Hartline was the crazed killer running wild in Arabella? On the other hand, what if there was no such person at all, that it was a carefully worked-out conspiracy of some sort, purpose unknown, and Hartline was a deadly tool being used to accomplish whatever the scheme involved? If that was the way of it then Gabe's attempts to kill him had been by intent, and at the direction of someone who had warned the gunslinger of his coming. But who—

Lark swore helplessly, brushed at the sweat on his face. It was all too deep, too mixed up with possibilities for him to come up with any answers, and he was almost sorry he'd taken the job when John Foreman offered it to him. But he had, and despite the uncomfortable feeling that he was in well over his head, he'd stick with it, not so much now for the wages involved but because a quitter was no part of his makeup.

Regardless, Lark decided he'd not close the book

on Gabe Hartline entirely as being the murderer, nor his possible connection with Reuben Cade, until he had more definite facts that would tie them to the killings. Odds were there was no connection —but he'd be smart, play it cozy and wait.

Prestridge reached Arabella late in the morning and rode directly to the stable behind the Bullhead Saloon. The sun was coming down hard and the buckskin was hot, and it would be better for him to wait in the cool of the barn until Lark was ready to use him again.

Crossing to the rear of the saloon, Prestridge entered and made his way through the eerily quiet room to where Gribble was washing glasses accumulated during the previous night's business. There was no one else around, and Lark reckoned the cowhands, the drummer and his woman, and the Fords had all gone their respective ways.

"You see Cade?" Phin asked, laying his towel aside as Prestridge halted at the bar. Selecting two clean glasses, the barman filled them with whiskey from a nearby bottle, slid one toward Lark and waited expectantly for an answer to his question.

"I did," Lark replied. "Sort of halfway claimed Hartline didn't work for him. Got the idea he was trying to protect him."

Gribble nodded. "Could've been. Gabe was sure working for him a few days ago."

Prestridge tossed off his drink. "Finally went ahead and admitted it all right."

"Reuben's kind of cagey most of the time. Sounds like he was being that way with you. You think he's got something to do with Gabe trying to shoot you?"

"I've done some wondering, but I've about made up my mind he don't. Can't see any reason why he would. They come up with the idea that Hartline—he's a hired gun, according to Cade—mistook me for somebody he'd been paid to kill."

Gribble, drink still untouched, grinned. "You swallow that hogwash? You ever hear of a hired gun making that kind of a mistake?"

Prestridge shrugged. "No, can't say as I have, and I'm not saying that I believe all that I heard out there at the Lazy C, either. I'm just trying to put it all together, add it up and make sense out of it. As far as Gabe Hartline's concerned, he still heads up my list as being the killer I'm looking for."

Gribble nodded. "And I'd sort of keep my eye on Reuben Cade, too, was I you."

Lark was studying his empty glass. He'd tipped his hand to the saloonman, but wasn't certain Phin had caught the slip—not that it really mattered now; he'd picked up just about all the incidental information possible.

"Reckon my hunch was right," he heard Gribble say. "You ain't no drifter passing through, are you?"

Prestridge stirred slightly, helped himself to another drink. Let Phin talk.

"You're some kind of a lawman—and you've come here to hunt down that murderer. Ain't that right?"

Lark nodded. "Was hired by the sheriff up at Kingdom City—John Foreman."

"You ain't a U.S. marshal?"

"Deputy sheriff—although I've never been any kind of a lawman before. Just happened I was in the same outfit with Foreman during the war, and he figured maybe I could get the job done. Didn't like fooling you, or anybody else, about who I was and why I'd come, but it seemed best until I could get the lay of the land and some idea of who my friends would be."

"Can savvy that," Phin said, and then swore softly. "You sure got yourself off to a good start —dang nigh getting ventilated by Gabe Hartline soon as you hit here!" The saloonman paused, rubbed at his neck. "You know what I'm wondering?"

Lark shook his head. He was relieved that Gribble knew his identity; he needed someone to talk to, someone to kick things back and forth with and sound out ideas on; Phin was ideal for the purpose.

"If there ain't nothing to Gabe's mistaking you for some jasper he'd been hired to kill—and that's plenty hard to believe—why'd he try so hard to cut you down? You ain't one of them sodbusters, and he sure knew it."

Prestridge, staring off through the open doorway at the distant, sun-flooded slopes, said, "For sure," and waited to see if the same thought occurred to the saloonkeeper that had come to him.

"Makes me believe Gabe knowed you was coming here, and why, and was told to put a bullet into you before you could start turning over any rocks and looking under them."

"Which would mean there's nothing to the idea that there's a crazy killer on the loose."

"Right. Would mean that Gabe's the killer, and that he'd been hired by somebody to do the killings."

Prestridge nodded. "I've been thinking the same thing, and if it's true there won't be any more murders unless whoever's back of it sends in a man to take Hartline's place." Lark hesitated, listened briefly to the sound of a running horse approaching the settlement. "You know anything about Cade's daughter, Martha?"

"Not much—'cepting she and her pa ain't very close. What're you wanting to know?"

"She married?"

"Nope, not far as can say. If she has got herself hitched, it would have been in the last month or so—and I would've heard about it. Why?"

"Mighty fine looker, and a nice girl—or I best say woman, I expect. She's probably in her middle twenties."

"Likely. Could be a couple years shy of that. Heading towards being an old maid."

"Man wonders why. She could sure have her choice of a lot of men—with all she's got to offer. There some reason she hasn't married?"

"Not that I know of. . . . What're you aiming to do next? Send word to the sheriff that you figure Gabe was the killer and that he's dead?"

"Got to do some looking around first, try and dig up some solid proof. No way I can tie him into the murders for sure yet. Appreciate your letting me talk it out with you, but I'm going to ask a favor."

"Yeh?"

"Keep what you know about me under your hat. Like for folks to keep on thinking I'm just some saddletramp for a while. Makes it easier to get around, ask questions."

"Sure thing. Say, you was asking about the Fords last night, and them being out. Well, it seems Linus and the boy was coming back from Crawfordsville. Been up seeing about selling off his corn crop, and the boy, Frank, was calling on a gal friend he's sweet on and's hoping to talk into marrying him. They got hung up and was running late."

"They stick around much after I turned in?"

"Hour or two. Never paid it no mind. Think I asked you this before, but you ain't been thinking they had a hand in them murders, are you?"

"No, not specially. Them being one of the families living around the lake—it wouldn't make much sense unless you'd figure Ford was getting hoggish and wanting more land—"

Lark broke off as a tall, gangling man dressed in a linsey-woolsey shirt, coarse pants and thick-soled farmer shoes came through the doorway. Straw hat in hand, sweat glistening on his forehead, he advanced hurriedly to the bar.

"Howdy, Carl," Phin greeted. "How're things down at the Lovens'?"

Carl shook his head, ran a hand agitatedly across his sun- and wind-burned features. "Give me a drink—"

Phin, frowning, produced a glass, filled it from the bottle on the counter, and passing it on to the man, glanced at Lark.

"Carl, here, works for Jim Loven, one of the homesteaders," he explained.

Carl, thick, stubby fingers enclosing the shot glass, brought it to his mouth and gulped a swallow of the liquor.

"Ain't there no more," he mumbled.

Gribble again cast a side look at Prestridge, brought his attention back to the hired man. "You saying you've quit Jim?"

"Quit—and leaving fast as I can," Carl said feelingly. "Work's mighty scarce, I hear, but I'll take my chances on finding me a job somewhere. Anything'll beat getting my head blowed off."

Lark came to attention. "Something happen that made you decide to pull out?"

Carl came half around, eyes still haunted by fear. "That killer—that's what happened! He shot Earl Ford dead this morning."

12

"Earl?" Gribble echoed. "Dead."

Carl bobbed, took another gulp of the whiskey. "Bullet went right through his heart. Reckon he never knowed what hit him."

Lark Prestridge was staring, unseeing, at the man, while thoughts accumulated swiftly in his head. Another murder—six now altogether. And what he had considered progress in the way of turning up the killer—the possibility that it was Gabe Hartline, or maybe Linus Ford and his son Frank—had suddenly disappeared like a puff of dust in the wind.

"When did it happen?" he asked in a sagging voice.

"Must've been about daylight, according to Linus. See, him and Frank had been off somewheres, and got home late, after midnight. The old man said he looked in on Earl, letting him know they was back, and then went on to bed."

"Earl was all right then around midnight?"

"Reckon so. Linus said they talked a bit. Slept

late, Frank said. Didn't get up till around six o'clock. The old man went outside for something, found Earl laying down by the barn—dead. He'd been—"

"Seems Frank or Linus would've heard the shot," Gribble murmured.

"Well, Frank says he thinks maybe he heard it but he ain't sure. Was sleeping, but it could've woke him up for just a second. . . . Was that loco killer again, sure'n hell. Too bad, too. Earl was a mighty nice boy."

"You get there right after they found him?" Lark asked.

Earl settled his eyes on Prestridge, frowned. "I don't recollect knowing you."

"Name's Lark Prestridge—friend of mine," Phin reassured him. "Can talk to him—he's trying to help."

"Nope, I didn't get there right away," Carl said, taking up Lark's question. "Was a couple hours, maybe three. I was up in Loven's north pasture, seen Frank digging on the side of that little hill where they've got a graveyard. Missus Ford's buried there, and so's the baby they lost to lung fever. First thing I thought was that the old man had passed away and Frank was digging a grave for him. Was same as getting kicked in the belly by a mule when he told me it was for Earl."

Silence hung in the saloon after that while each man considered his own thoughts. Finally Phin Gribble broke the hush.

"Expect Linus is taking it mighty hard."

"He sure is. Just stood around while me and Frank laid Earl away, looking off towards the lake and mumbling to himself now and then. When we was done he told us to go, leave him be. We did and when I looked back I seen him a-setting on the grave—just setting there like he was thinking. . . . Phin, you reckon Nellie can fix me up a bite of lunch?"

The saloonman said, "Sure. I'll go tell her now," and moved out from behind the counter.

"Won't need nothing fancy, just something that'll hold me for a couple of days while I'm on the trail."

Gribble nodded and Carl, lifting his glass, drained the last of his drink. Lark reached for the bottle, slid it toward the man.

"Have another one—on me."

The hired man smiled tightly, accepted the proffered refill. "I'm obliged, Mr. Prestridge."

"Just Lark. Don't think I got your last name—"

"It's Lindquist. Carl Lindquist."

"Good Scandinavian name. . . . You and the Fords figure out where the shot that killed Earl came from?"

Carl took a sip of his drink. His taut manner had eased considerably now, and the anxiety had all but faded from his eyes.

"Well, me and Frank done some scouting around. Damn killer had to be hiding in a stand of brush off to the right—that'd be the north—of the house."

"How far away would that be?"

Carl frowned, glanced toward the restaurant as the sound of Phin Gribble returning reached him. "Oh, I reckon it's a good hundred yards—maybe even a bit more."

"Rifle," Prestridge murmured thoughtfully. "And the man using it knows how. You find an empty cartridge or anything?"

"Nope. Was a place where the weeds was tromped down."

"How about hoofprints?"

"Weren't none. We thought of that, too—of maybe tracking his horse—but there wasn't nothing to track."

"Probably left his horse off to the side a ways," Gribble said, coming in on the last of the conversation as he resumed his customary place behind the counter. "Nellie said she'd have you all fixed up time you're ready to go."

Lindquist nodded, said, "Sure am obliged," and laid a silver dollar on the bar.

"Drinks are on the house," Phin said, pushing the coin back. "Can settle with Nellie for your grub. Got any idea which way you'll be going?"

"Nope, just aim to get a far piece from here. All this killing with nobody doing anything about it—it's enough to turn a man's heart sour."

"Nobody's been able to do anything, Carl," Phin said quietly. "There just hasn't been anything to go on."

"Yeh, I know that, but—"

"You've been here during all five—now it's six—of the murders," Lark said. "Did you ever see anything that gave you an idea or a hunch who it might be?"

Elbows on the bar, Carl twirled his empty glass between a thumb and forefinger, thought deeply. "No sir, sure didn't."

"Like a man on foot carrying a rifle, walking along the lake or through the brush. Wouldn't have to be a stranger—could be somebody you know."

"Somebody living here in town—or maybe on one of the farms?" Lindquist said in a surprised voice as if realizing that possibility for the first time.

"Right. Could even be your best friend."

Carl began to wag his head slowly. "Can't go by none of that," he said. "Since the killings started just about everybody around here's carrying a gun —and far as folks out walking, they don't do no more'n they just have to in getting their work done." The man paused, looked more closely at Lark. "You a lawman come here to find out who the killer is?"

"The killer took a shot at him last night," Phin said, avoiding a direct answer to the question Lindquist had put to Prestridge. "We all thought the fellow was the killer, I mean. Looks like we figured wrong."

"How so?" Lindquist asked, starting to move toward the restaurant area.

"Lark killed him when he tried a second time to bushwhack him. That was early evening. If he'd been the murderer he wouldn't have been around to kill Earl this morning."

"I see," Carl said. "I know the fellow?"

"Name's Gabe Hartline. Cowhand that's been working for Reuben Cade," Prestridge replied. "You ever see him around the lake?"

◎ 13 ◎

Lark Prestridge rode south out of town, using as much care as possible to not expose himself any more than necessary. The killer was still alive and free, and although Lark kept to the shelter of the brush he was uncomfortably aware that a bullet could reach him at any moment despite his precautions.

Why Gabe Hartline had sought to kill him continued to be a puzzling question in his mind as he bore steadily for Arabella Lake, but the explanation advanced by Martha Cade—that the gunman mistook him for another man—had now assumed stronger logic. But that was around the bend, and there was little gained in hashing it over.

The first homestead he'd come to, Gribble had said, would be the Gunderson's. Al Gunderson himself was dead, the first victim of the murderer; his widow, Charity, with two small daughters to raise, was endeavoring to keep the place going.

Lark caught sight of Gunderson's not long after

the lake, shimmering in the bright sunlight, came into view. Halting on a knoll, he pulled off his hat, wiped away the accumulation of sweat on his forehead and studied the collection of structures: main house, barn, feed sheds, wagon lean-tos, and other lesser buildings grouped in a clearing. All appeared in good repair.

The crop of corn, melons, vegetables, hay and fruit, all laid out in orderly plots and rows, looked rich and healthy, gave promise of a fine harvest. But there were signs of deterioration. Here and there weeds had begun to encroach, and there were broken places in the ditches fluming water in from the lake for irrigation. Over on the east side of the cornfield, a section of the rail fence was down. Lark didn't know how long it had been since Gunderson was shot to death, but before many more weeks passed the homestead would be showing a marked change for the worse. A farm required constant maintenance, and with no man present or available to see to such, Charity Gunderson faced a serious problem.

Replacing his hat, Lark raked the buckskin with his spurs, sent him moving off the low hill and down toward the clearing. As he angled more to the side he provided himself with a better view of the yard. A buckboard was standing at the rack near the front of the house. Two small girls, probably eight and ten years of age, played nearby. There was a well with a pump, a flower bed now suffering from neglect, clumps of dusty shrubs, a table with several chairs, all crudely built, and a line from which hung freshly washed clothes.

It was a quiet, peaceful scene, one unrelated to the fear and tragedy that stalked the lush, green country of Arabella Lake. Watching, Prestridge frowned. The two small girls had suddenly abandoned their play, were running to the house. Something had frightened them. Lark drew the Henry from its boot, laid it across his legs, all the while probing the edge of the yard for movement. It could be the killer—

The spiteful crack of a rifle, a spurt of dust and litter on the trail directly ahead of him brought Lark up short. Realization rushed through him—Charity Gunderson was shooting at him. She evidently had spotted him coming down the slope, and alarmed at the sight of a stranger, which was to be expected, she'd opened up. Grinning tightly, he slid his weapon back into the leather.

"Hold your fire!" he called. "I'm—"

The rifle cracked again. The bullet buried itself in a stump a bit to his right—and close.

"Mrs. Gunderson!" he shouted. "I'm a deputy! Sheriff sent me. Name's Prestridge. Like to talk to you."

No third shot came from the house and silence prevailed while the woman apparently gave his words consideration. Finally her answer came.

"How do I know the sheriff sent you? Could be a lie—a trick—"

"No ma'am, nothing like that," Lark said. "I've got a letter from Sheriff Foreman. If you'll let me ride in I'll show it to you. Wants me to try and run down whoever killed your husband—and the others. And Phin Gribble up in town can vouch for me."

Again there was a quiet, broken by the distant singing of a mockingbird, the quacking of ducks on the lake, the nearby clicking of insects in the brush.

"All right, mister!" Charity's answer, coming at

last, was firm, specific. "Come on in—but keep your hands where I can see them. There'll be a rifle pointing at you all the way. One wrong move and you're dead. Understand?"

"Yes'm," Lark said, a hard smile on his lips, and started the buckskin downslope again.

He came to the edge of the hardpack, walked the horse onto it slowly. Both his hands were resting on the saddlehorn in plain view as he slanted for the front of the house. He could see the woman standing in the shadows a few steps back inside the doorway. She had her rifle leveled at him. Drawing abreast, Lark halted, looked at her expectantly.

"Climb down," he heard her say. "Be mighty careful, now!"

Prestridge, palms still on the horn, swung off the saddle, settled himself squarely on his feet, and then, withdrawing his hands and holding them up, faced the door.

"Throw that pistol you're wearing off to the side," she directed.

Lark shook his head. "Nope, I draw the line there. The way things are around these parts, I could need it fast."

Charity Gunderson gave that thought. "All right," she said. "Just keep standing there with your arms raised while I have a look at that letter you were talking about."

She came to the doorway, pushed open the dust-clogged screen and stepped out onto the porch. Around thirty, Lark reckoned, she was a solidly built but not a heavy woman with reddish hair, a fair skin and light eyes. That she had once been most attractive was certain, for it still showed in her face and the contours of her body despite the weight of toil.

"Where's this letter?" she demanded, her lips set to a firm line.

"Shirt pocket," Lark replied. "You'll find my star there, too. . . . I'll be obliged if you'll be a mite careful with that rifle. You've got the hammer pulled back."

"It's going to stay that way, too," Charity snapped, raising the weapon slightly. The muzzle was almost touching his belly as she probed for the letter. Finding it, and the star, she stepped back. The star fell from her fingers as she struggled to open the envelope.

"Damn," she muttered, and moved another step away.

"Put your gun down, lady," Prestridge said indifferently. "I could've grabbed the barrel and taken it away from you anytime I wanted."

Charity considered him coldly, eyes half closed, lips still compressed. There was a determined set to her jaw, and he reckoned if he had tried to disarm her, it would have been no easy chore. But his words had their desired effect, and hanging her weapon in the crook of an elbow—the hammer still at full-cock position—she removed the sheet of paper John Foreman had written on from its envelope and quickly read it. Finished, she looked up.

"I reckon you're who the letter says you are, unless you stole it from the real Lark Prestridge—killed him."

There was a note of hopeless desperation in Charity Gunderson's voice, as if she wanted to believe but, disappointed by experience, was afraid to do so. It was understandable; the woman had been through hell—and it wasn't over for her yet.

"I'm Prestridge, all right," Lark assured her

gently. "I've got nothing else on me that I can use to prove it. You figure if I was out to do you harm I'd come riding down that hill wide open—like I was?"

Charity shrugged. Handing the letter back to him, she released the hammer on her rifle and propped the weapon against one of the porch roof supports. Retrieving his star from the loose dust, she tossed it to him.

"No, I suppose not," she said. "But I've learned, like everybody else around here, to take no chances. It just seems there's no safety, no protection any more for us—"

"Why I'm here," Lark said as her voice broke slightly. "I'm hoping you can give me some help so I can put an end to the trouble down here."

"He's killed again," the woman said heavily. "Shot—murdered Earl Ford this morning."

"Heard about it," Prestridge said, pinning the star to his shirt where it could be seen. Judging from the state of mind Charity Gunderson was in, he could expect everyone else along the lake to be edgy and suspicious. Wearing his badge instead of keeping it hidden in a pocket not only would be prudent but would also eliminate much explaining.

The woman took a corner of her faded, checked apron, dabbed at the moisture on her cheeks and forehead.

"What is it you want to know?" she asked.

"Everything you can tell me about your husband's murder," Lark said, and pausing there watched Charity closely to see what reaction the mentioning of Al Gunderson's death brought.

There was no change in her—no tears, no blinking of eyes, only a slight tightening in the planes of her face. Gunderson's widow had long since stood up to her loss, adjusted, and was meeting the future as best she could, he guessed.

"All right," Charity said, turning to the door. "Let's go inside, sit down out of the heat. Won't take long to tell you what little I know."

14

Reclaiming her rifle, Charity Gunderson pulled open the screen door, took a final precautionary look around as Prestridge withdrew the Henry from its boot, and then, followed by him, entered the low-roofed house.

It was a large room and served as general living quarters for the family, he saw. There were curtain-covered archways leading into adjoining bedrooms and the kitchen. As Lark drew to a halt just inside, the woman motioned him to a square table at one end.

"Take a chair. Coffee's on the stove. I'll fetch it."

Prestridge settled on one of the four straight-back chairs placed around the table, smiled at the pair of youngsters considering him shyly from the entrance to the kitchen.

"The redhead's Maggie," Charity said, brushing past them with cups and a pot of coffee in her hands. "Other one's Mary. They don't especially look it, but they're twins." Halting, she sat down opposite Lark, nodded to the girls. "Run play now, but mind you, stay right close to the front door."

"Yes, Mama," Maggie said, and hurried across the room with Mary at her heels.

Charity watched them skip the last few steps, bang the screen door shut as they rushed into the yard, and shook her head.

"They don't really understand what's happened," she said, filling the cups. "They're only ten—not even that yet, actually. Be another month."

"One good thing about being young," Lark said, drawing his coffee toward him. Taking it up, he sipped at the thick, black liquid, swallowed and nodded slightly. "Good."

Charity smiled. "Too much chicory—and you know it—but I've got to make my coffee beans stretch. What is it you want to know about my husband?"

Lark took another swig of the bitter brew, set his cup aside. "Like to know how it happened, first of all."

The woman leaned back in her chair, stared off through the open doorway. "Al was out in the field, was opening one of the ditches intending to irrigate the corn. I was doing some baking, heard a gunshot. I walked over to the window and looked out. He was coming toward the house, staggering, trying to reach here before he fell. He went to his knees right about then. I ran out there to him, but he was already dead when I got to his side."

Charity's recital had been composed, matter-of-fact, but Lark could see the wound in her soul ran deep, and it was sheer will power that kept her on an even keel.

"You got any idea where the shot came from?"

The woman shrugged. "From the trees and the brush, I'd guess."

"Same way that Earl Ford was bushwhacked—"

"And Tom Lockwood and poor Charley White and Ben Wilson. They were all out in the field, working. The murderer hid in the bushes and shot them—was from quite a ways. Nobody even got a look at him—not even a little glimpse. . . . How long have you been in town?"

"Got in yesterday."

"Surprised you don't already know all about what's been happening."

"I've got a pretty fair idea. You ever hear of a man named Gabe Hartline?"

Charity frowned, considered the coffee in her cup as she sloshed it gently about. "Not sure. May sound familiar, but I can't pin it down."

"Been working for Reuben Cade, up at the Lazy C. I thought for a time he was your loco killer, and that the trouble you folks have been having down here was over."

"What made you think that?"

"Hartline tried to kill me—tried twice, in fact, for no real reason except murder. I had to shoot him. Everything seemed to point to him as the man who's been doing the killing around here. Then I heard that Earl Ford had been shot this morning—and that ruled out Hartline as the murderer. He was dead not long after dark last night."

"I see. You say he worked for the Cades?"

"Did—at one time, anyway. But we can forget about him."

"I suppose, but if he wasn't the maniac that's been murdering people around here, why'd he want to kill you?"

Lark warmed the remaining coffee in his cup

from the pot. "Only thing we could come up with was that he took me for somebody else—somebody he was hired to kill."

Charity rose, walked to the door, glanced about. Satisfied, she returned to her chair. "That's possible, I suppose," she murmured. Then, "Have you talked to any of the other homesteaders along the lake?"

He shook his head. "Did meet Linus Ford and his son Frank last night. We didn't talk."

"Well, the place south of us—we're at the west end of the lake, in case you're twisted around—belonged to the Lockwoods. Tom was killed about three or four days after my husband, Al. Was the same way—shot from the brush while he was working. The place is deserted now. Willa, Tom's wife—or I should say widow—packed up their four little kids and moved away. Said she couldn't stand to stay there any longer.

"On east of Lockwood's is Galen Hill. Nothing's happened there—yet—but Galen's expecting it and I think he's going to pull out, too."

There was a faint edge to the woman's words, as if she held the man in contempt for entertaining thoughts of following a course she apparently considered cowardly.

"The Lovens are on east of him—Jim and Amy. They say they're not going to quit, that they'll not be scared off—and the killer be damned. Both of them go around armed all the time—Jim with a pistol and rifle, Amy with the shotgun she used to hunt quail and rabbits with."

"Going armed's not much help if you never get a look at the man shooting at you."

"What I said, too, and I expect they realize that, but it doesn't matter. Just some comfort in going around with a gun under your arm. . . . Linus Ford and his boys—boy—live north of them, at the east end of the lake. Be just Linus and Frank now."

"There's no Mrs. Ford, I understand."

"No, Linus' wife died years ago, not long after they came here. Heard Frank was about to marry some girl up Crawfordsville way, but it never come from him so I don't know if there's anything to it or not. I don't know the Fords very well. Linus has always been sort of odd, and the boys've always kept to themselves."

"Who's in the place above them—that'll be the northeast corner of the lake?"

Charity nodded. "You're getting your directions straight quick. That's where Levi Trent lived."

"Lived? He the other man that's been killed?"

"Yes," Charity said, and again rising and walking to the door, had her look about. Resuming her seat, she continued. "He lived there alone, except for help he hired now and then. Never tried very hard to make his place pay, just sort of rocked along, taking it easy. Was grieving over something, folks all figured—maybe a wife or a woman he'd hoped to make his wife, only didn't."

"The murderer shoot him from the brush like he did the others?"

"No, was different. From the way it looked the killer must've watched him for a spell, learned he lived there alone. They found Levi laying on the floor of his kitchen. He'd been called to the door, and when he opened it, got himself shot—at least that's the way Galen Hill and the others figured it happened. Place is deserted now, same as Lockwood's and Ed Minton's—on to the west of Trent's."

"Minton move on, too, like Mrs. Lockwood?"

"Yes, right after they found poor old Levi. Ed was getting pretty nervous even before that, however, and I'd been expecting him to run. I wasn't much surprised when I found out he'd packed up his family and belongings and pulled out."

Lark pushed his cup toward the coffee pot. The bitter combination of ground chicory root and coffee beans would be cold, he knew, but it didn't matter. In the yard he could hear the happy, excited voices of Maggie and Mary Gunderson, uninhibited by the danger that stalked Arabella Lake, playing at their childish games.

"Means there's three abandoned homesteads."

"Three up to now—before Earl Ford's death. That could cause the Hills to leave. . . . This coffee's cold. I'll heat it if you like."

"Never mind. . . . If they do then only you and the Lovens and the Fords will be left."

"Just us," Charity said, brushing a wisp of hair back from her face. "Doubt if either of them will ever run—have to kill them to get them off their land. Same goes for me—not that I'm not scared. Just don't have anyplace I could go."

Prestridge had come forward at the woman's words, his square, browned face taut. "You said *off their land*. That mean somebody's been around offering to buy?"

Charity Gunderson shook her head. "Didn't mean to give you that idea, just a way of saying it. Now, I can't speak for the others, but far as Al and I are concerned—or were—nobody ever offered to buy us out. Leastwise, not that I know of. If somebody talked to Al about it he didn't mention it to me."

"But that's not saying for sure somebody didn't.

Your husband could've just figured it wasn't worth mentioning, or simply forgot."

Charity nodded, said, "I guess so—but I still doubt it. Anyway, I don't see what that's got to do with it. The killer is some kind of a crazy man. That's what I think, what everybody thinks."

"Seems to be the idea in town, too," Prestridge said, "and I'm not disagreeing, only digging into every angle."

"He's somebody that hates homesteaders—maybe a hired hand who once worked around here."

"Could be."

Charity fell silent as Lark sat staring thoughtfully through the doorway. Outside the little girls continued their playing, busily chattering all the while.

"I help you any?" the woman asked.

"Plenty," Prestridge replied, although, in truth, he'd acquired only more generalities and nothing concrete that he could go on. "Was just thinking I ought to talk to the other homesteaders, too, see if they can come up with anything."

"Be a right good idea, only—"

"Only what? If you think I'm scared the killer—"

"Not that. Always before there's been a few days between the murders, like he knew everybody'd be on guard for a while, and he'd lay back until they eased off. No, I was thinking I'd best go with you —for that very reason. A stranger riding across the fields or coming down the road could get himself shot—like you almost did a bit ago."

Prestridge grinned. "Hadn't considered that, but there's a lot of truth in it. There a chance you could find the time, Mrs. Gunderson?"

"Charity," she cut in, "and I'll call you Lark. Can't think of your other name."

"Prestridge."

"Yeh, I remember now. It all right if I call you Lark?"

"Of course."

"Fine. . . . It's near noon. I'll fix us a bite of dinner, then we can leave. I'll have to drop my girls at the Hills'—we'll be talking to them first."

"I don't want to put you to any trouble."

"No trouble. You stay right where you are, or look around while I get things ready," Charity said, moving toward the kitchen. "Just make yourself at home."

15

An hour later they rolled out of the Gunderson yard, following the twin tracks in the grassy sod that led to the adjoining Lockwood place. Charity held the reins of the big, bucket-hoofed bay that did double duty at the plow and the buckboard.

With the two little girls riding in the bed, Lark Prestridge, rifle across his knees, sat beside the woman. He was nervous and uneasy and maintained a constant roving surveillance of the country for signs of danger, and long before they reached the abandoned Lockwood farm, he was having regrets.

"I don't like this," he said, heavily. "Was wrong of me to drag you out into the open—make it easy for that murderer to—"

"About as safe here as being around the house," Charity interrupted. "Specially having a man along."

Prestridge shrugged. He doubted his presence would make any difference to a man standing off in the thick brush with a rifle.

"When we get to where you aim to leave your girls, best you stay there, too. I can go on alone."

Charity's mouth was a firm line. "And get yourself shot. No, I'll show you around. . . . There's the Lockwood place."

Lark followed her pointing finger. The peaked roofs of a house and barn were showing beyond a wooded rise to their right. As they swung around the hillock and drew nearer, he saw more of the farm—the smaller, cruder sheds, the fenced yards, corrals and pens. Neglect was already having its way with them, and weeds were taking over the gardens and beginning to choke the fields, bleached brown for lack of water.

"Doesn't take long for things to go down," Charity said quietly. "Another month and Tom's place will look like nobody's worked it for years."

Lark agreed. Then, "Too bad some of the other homesteaders don't throw in together and take over the place. Could share the crop. Letting it go to waste's a shame."

"Nobody's got the time," the woman explained. "Hired help's all pulled out, scared off by the murders. Folks have all got their hands full trying to keep up with their own places. . . . You want to stop?"

Prestridge said, "No point. Nobody there to talk to. What will happen to the Lockwood farm?"

Charity slapped the broad back of the bay with slack reins, kept him ambling steadily along the faintly marked road.

"Caroline—Tom's widow—is hoping somebody will come along, make an offer for it. She left the papers with Hotchkiss, in town," Charity replied, and then glanced at him. "Why? You interested in it?"

There was a note of hope in the woman's voice, and her eyes brightened. But the light faded immediately as Lark shook his head.

"No, just wondering," Prestridge said, making mental note of what she had said about the store owner. It might pay to see how deep the interest of Hotchkiss went in the property lying around Arabella Lake. "What are your plans? I don't see how you can keep a big place like yours going without help."

"I'll manage," Charity said confidently. "I'm not going to try and save all my crop—only what I can. And next year, if I'm still alive, I won't plant any more than it'll take to keep the girls and me—I'm not faced by a big mortgage or any debts, so it won't take much. Of course, if things change and you run down this killer, we'll all be able to get hired hands again."

They rode on through the pleasant, if hot, day. Ducks were continuing to make their presence known on the lake, a peaceful-looking circle of sky-mirroring blue water off to their left. Here and there cattle grazed, and Lark saw a small flock of sheep, being raised, no doubt, for their wool rather than their meat.

High overhead two broad-tailed hawks soared tirelessly back and forth as they hunted, and well off to the north, beyond the lake, a dog barked forlornly. Charity listened for a time as the bay trotted on and the iron tired wheels of the buckboard cut smoothly through the grass.

"That's Ed Minton's dog," she said, after a time. "He won't leave the place. I'd like to have him but there's no getting him to come. Tried twice but he just stood there, looked at me."

"Could throw a rope on him."

"Would mean I'd have to keep him chained up, and I won't do that. I need a good dog—a couple, maybe, like the pair we had that ran off—to run loose in the yard and keep out the varmints."

Lark smiled. Charity Gunderson showed no fear of the future despite the fact she'd lost her husband to a killer, had two small daughters to rear, a hundred and sixty acres of farm to look after—and the possibility that now she would become the objective of the murderer. He swore quietly under his breath at the woman's courage, vowed that if for no other reason than to help her, he'd track down the bushwhacker and make it possible for her to continue life in peace.

The Galen Hill farm was a model of orderliness. As they pulled into the yard Lark could not but notice the broad hardpack, as clean and litter-free as if it had been broom-swept, the trimmed bushes and shrubbery, the snow-white trunks of the numerous trees, limed to a height of six feet or so.

The house was in excellent repair from outside appearances, but the barn, as was so often the case among farmers, was a fine, strongly built structure that by far outshone the residence. Boasting a coat of paint not too long since applied, it approximated the size of most town livery stables, had wide double doors facing the yard as well as one of standard size that opened into a tack room built in one corner. Two large windows, open now for ventilation, were in the south wall, and undoubtedly there would be doors and more windows at the rear of the structure, as well as rooms for storage, stalls for horses and cows, and a loft, all under the one roof.

"Hill's got himself a fine place," Lark said,

as the buckboard rolled to a stop at the rear of the house.

"He's a good farmer," Charity replied, and looked to the door, swinging open.

A thin woman in a housedress and apron, gray-streaked hair pulled to the back of her head, brown features sharp but pleasant, came out onto the porch.

"Charity!" she called, wiping her hands on a square of cloth and smiling. "It's good to see you!"

At the sound of her voice several small children came pouring noisily out of the building, crowding past her, shouting at the Gunderson girls as they did. Both Mary and Maggie instantly leaped from the bed of the buckboard and raced off with the Hill offspring toward what was apparently a favored play area beneath a large cottonwood.

"Patience," Charity said when the noise and confusion had moved beyond earshot, "this is Lark Prestridge. He's a deputy the sheriff sent down here to catch that murderer. This is Mrs. Hill, Lark."

Prestridge nodded, touched the brim of his hat to the woman, who smiled, said, "Glad to know you."

"I'd like to leave the girls with you while I take him around, introduce him to the rest of the folks," Charity said.

The smile on Patience Hill's lips curved downward into a grimace. "Rest," she echoed wearily. "Not counting you and us, there's only the Lovens and the Fords left—and only two of them. You heard about Earl, I reckon."

Charity said, "Yes—but maybe that will be the last murder we'll hear about now that we've got somebody looking into it. . . . Where's your husband? Lark would like to ask him some questions."

Patience pointed off to the south. "Working the corn. . . . Will the girls be staying the night?"

"No, we'll be back by late this afternoon. I hope you don't mind—"

"Mind? I should say not. Keeps my younguns out from under my feet," Patience said and nodded to Lark. "Glad to've met you."

"Same here," Prestridge replied, and again touched the brim of his hat as Charity cut the buckboard around sharply and headed off toward Hill's lower field.

They found the homesteader resting in the shade of a tree placed strategically, and probably intentionally, at a corner of the field. Hill was probably in his mid-forties, a short, wiry blond with a thick mustache and ragged beard. He was wearing bib overalls, heavy shoes, a patched, faded blue shirt and a wide-brimmed flat-crowned hat. He had small, intense, agatelike eyes but there was a weariness to him, as if he were about ready to give in.

Charity made the introductions, then cast an appraising glance at the long rows of corn standing straight in the driving sunlight.

"Looks like you're going to have a fine crop this year, Galen."

"What I'm hoping for," Hill said. "You hear about Earl Ford, Deputy?"

Lark said, "I have. You notice anybody around that might've had a hand in the shooting—stranger or otherwise?"

"Nope, and I've been up and about since four o'clock. With no help me and the missus have to do everything ourselves."

"Guess nobody has any hired help since Carl

Lindquist left the Lovens," the woman said. "Have you talked to Linus?"

"No, ain't had time. Got my own family to look after, anyway. Soon as the harvest's in and I've sold off, I'm packing up the family and leaving."

Charity frowned. "Then you've made up your mind for sure?"

"Yeh, did this morning after hearing about Earl. You say you want to ask me about that maniac?" Hill added, turning to Lark. "I can't tell you nothing because I don't know nothing. Whoever he is, he's like a damned ghost. Comes and goes without nobody ever getting a look at him. Does his shooting from the brush."

"What I've been told," Prestridge said. "There been anybody around wanting to buy your place?"

Hill gave that a minute's thought. "No, ain't never been. Was a jasper here about a year ago talking corn. Wanted to buy my crop—rancher, I think he was. He's the only one. That what you're looking for—somebody wanting the land and trying to drive us all off?"

"I'm trying to figure everything—anything, in fact, that might put me on the right track."

"Well, it ain't nothing like that. It's some kill-crazy fool, shooting down folks just for the hell of it. And for my part I'm getting my family out of here soon as I can. I'm not about to make the mistake Tom Lockwood did—get myself killed and put my wife and kids in the bind his are in the way he did—"

"And the way my Al did," Charity finished. "Go ahead, Galen, say it. Doesn't bother me because he couldn't have known it would work out this way."

"Don't mean to be bad-mouthing him, Charity,

it's just that I'm trying not to let it happen to me and my family. But I'm worried plenty. I've got this feeling that it ain't going to work out the way I hope—and I'm plumb helpless to do anything about it."

"Expect everybody pretty much feels the same way," the woman said, "but I've got a different feeling now."

The homesteader fixed her with questioning eyes. "Meaning what?"

"That we've got a man down here, finally, who's trying to track down the killer—and that's something we've never had before. What's more, I think he's going to get the job done."

Hill's lips pulled into a tight line. "I'm hoping so," he said. "Sunk everything, including my whole life, almost, into this place, and I sure hate to think about walking off, leaving it just when it's starting to pay off real good. . . . There anything I can do, Deputy?"

"Keep your eyes peeled," Lark said, and motioned for Charity to drive on.

16

They reached Loven's a short time later, found the homesteader standing in the doorway of his home, a rifle in his hands.

"Figured that was you coming up the lane, Charity," he said, putting the weapon aside, "but was kind of doubting, seeing a man there on the seat, too."

"His name's Lark Prestridge," said the woman, making the introductions, and as the men shook hands, she added, "He's a deputy. Been sent here by the sheriff to get that killer."

Loven shifted the cud of tobacco in his mouth to one cheek. A tall, hawk-faced man, he, like Hill, was in overalls, heavy shoes and wide-brimmed hat designed to keep off the sun, but unlike Galen Hill, he wore a full cartridge belt and a holstered pistol.

"About time the guv'ment was doing something," he said in an angry, impatient tone. "Been another killing this morning."

"We've heard about it," Charity said.

Lark was studying the man closely. After a bit he said, "You see anybody hanging around, or riding by that you didn't know—either this morning or yesterday?"

"Nope, nobody," Loven replied, "and if that's how you aim to catch that lunatic, you're plain wasting time. He ain't never let nobody see him, and by now he knows who you are and that you're hunting him—so he for dang sure ain't ever going to give you a look-see."

"Got to start somewhere," Prestridge said with a shrug. "Like to ask you the same question I've been asking the others. Has there been anybody around wanting to buy you out?"

Loven splattered the dust with tobacco juice, swiped at the sweat on his lined face with the back of a hand. "Nope, ain't nobody come talking to me. Expect you got the same answer from everybody else."

Prestridge nodded. Jim Loven swore, again spat. "Figured as much—and you're barking up the wrong tree, Deputy! It ain't somebody wanting our land, it's some crazy loon with a hankering to shed blood—homesteaders' blood."

"You recollect any hired hands you had trouble with?"

Loven looked off toward the lake, scratched at the gray stubble on his jaw. "Hired help comes and goes. Just about every year I'd be working somebody I never seen before. Have to push them all to get a day's work done—but I can't think of none that left here mad. . . . Reminds me, Charity. I said I'd send Lindquist over to give you a little help. Can't. He pulled out this morning."

"I know, Jim. Carl stopped and said goodbye."

"I'm mighty sorry about it. Are you doing all-right?"

The woman nodded. "Getting by. Place is going down. Just can't keep up with the work, so I do the things that have to be done, pass up the ones that ought to be."

"Know what you mean."

"We stopped by Galen's. He says he's packing up and leaving soon as he gets his crop in. You changed your mind any?"

Once again Loven spat a stream of brown juice. "Nope, I ain't leaving! Nothing's driving me off my farm—not after all the sweat I've put into it! I'll fight the devil hisself for what's mine!"

"Way I feel about my place," the woman said. "Al and I worked hard to make it what it is. I wouldn't be doing right by him if I quit."

Paying only half a mind to the conversation, Lark let his gaze probe the brush lying between the homesteader's yard and the lake, drift on to take on the slopes visible beyond. They could be in danger, exposed as they were there in the open, and he had an uncomfortable feeling that they were being watched. The previous murders had occurred while the man involved was working in his field, he recalled, and then remembered, also, that there had been an exception: Levi Trent. There was no hard-and-fast pattern, he guessed; it was a matter of opportunity for the killer.

"I wished you was a mite closer to us," he heard Loven say. "Living way off there at the other end of the lake makes it kind of hard to keep an eye on you. Amy was saying only last night that maybe we ought to talk you into bringing the girls and staying here with us for a time. Makes more sense that ever now that we've got a deputy on the job."

Charity Gunderson smiled, took up the slack in the bay's reins. "I appreciate the offer, Jim, but we'll make out all right. . . . There anything else you want to ask, Lark?"

"One thing—I just remembered," Prestridge said. "Came across a dead horse when I was riding in. A big gray. Didn't look like there was anything wrong with him—at least I couldn't see it if there was. He'd been shot in the head."

Loven nodded. "Sounds like Levi Trent's horse, or one of them he owned. Where'd you see him?"

Prestridge looked toward the hills, got his bearings. "Be north of here, and a bit east, maybe."

"Probably belonged to Trent, all right. That's up in his neck of the woods. Why?"

"Just wondered if it tied in with the murders."

"You bet it does!" Loven snapped. "Been quite a bit of stock killing going on. Some fields been fired, too, hay gone up in smoke. I ain't lost nothing that way yet—and I don't think you have either, Charity—but Trent and Ed Minton and the Cords all have. Just a matter of time now, I expect, until we get a taste of it, too. . . . That's a fine-looking gun you've got there, Deputy. Henry repeater, ain't it?"

Lark nodded. "Like to ask you to keep your eyes open for anybody that don't belong around here—or maybe that does but's not where he ought to be. If you see somebody get in touch with me. I'm staying at Phin Gribble's."

Loven snorted. "Time I could get word to you there, the fellow could be clear across the county line, but I'll be doing all I can. Where you all headed now?"

"Ford's," Charity said, lifting the lines.

"I see. Amy's baking up some bread and a pie

or two for Linus and Frank. I'll be obliged if you'll tell them we'll be along later."

"I will," the woman said, putting the bay into motion. "And you can tell Amy hello for me."

The buckboard moved on through the band of brush and trees separating Loven's fields from Arabella Lake. After a time Charity sighed.

"You're not getting much help," she said. "The answers to the questions you ask don't mean anything."

"Got to admit that's true," Lark said, "but I am getting a first-hand, close-up look at the people that're connected to the trouble."

Charity gave him a quick, puzzled glance. "You saying you think one of them might be the murderer? That the main reason you're doing this?"

"Far as I'm concerned, it could be any one of them, same as it might be somebody in town, but I doubt it. But if they're all telling the truth, there's been nobody around wanting to buy their homesteads, and that rules out somebody after the land."

"They're telling you the truth!" Charity said, a note of indignation in her tone. "Why shouldn't they? Why would they lie about it?"

"If they were in with somebody outside of the valley who was scheming to get all the land along the lake, they would. But I've already said I doubt that—not meaning, however, that I'm forgetting about it. Just seems, though, that you and the others all thinking it's some kind of a loony doing it could be right. What would help there is if somebody could remember firing a hired hand, and he pulled out mad, swearing to get even. But nobody can."

"It's sort of the other way around," Charity said.

"Folks are good to their help, because dependable hands are plenty hard to get in this country. No man wants to work for a sodbuster—they all want to punch cows, ride a horse."

"Kind of the way I feel, too," Lark said.

Working a field, hanging onto the handles of a plow and doing the other tedious, back-breaking chores that came with farming never had appealed to him; he would take the long hours in a saddle, the fence riding, the chousing cattle out of the brakes, the trail driving any time to the lot of a homesteader.

But most of the time a job was a job, and welcome. He was grateful to be working as a deputy at the moment, after which there was the possibility that he'd be hired by Reuben Cade to ride for the Lazy C, and there was that half-promise John Foreman had made about continuing to work for him—probably as a deputy. Of the two he'd prefer to sign on with Cade.

Lark's thoughts came to a sudden halt. Motion ahead and on their right had caught his eye. Charity had seen it, too. She brought the buckboard to an abrupt stop as Prestridge, Henry up and ready in his hands, probed the brush. He heard the woman sigh with relief.

"It's only Frank Ford," she said and raised her hand to the partly concealed figure in the growth. "Frank—it's me—Charity Gunderson!"

Ford lowered the double-barreled shotgun he had leveled, came slowly into view. Barely nodding to the woman, he considered Lark coldly.

"I know you from somewhere?"

"Last night—at the Bullhead. The shooting."

Ford's taut figure relented. "Yeh, I remember. What do you want?"

"I'm working for the sheriff. Sent me down here to put a stop to the killings. . . . Sorry to hear about your brother."

Frank shrugged. "Yeh," he said, and then continued, "Reckon I was wrong, thinking that fellow you shot was the killer—Hartline I think his name was."

"Seems he wasn't."

"Well, he was sure aiming to kill you. You ever figure out why?"

"Mistook me for somebody else, near as I can come to explaining it. You turn up anything that might tell us who it was that shot your brother?"

Frank shook his head. "Done a lot of looking around—me and Carl Lindquist—right after it happened, and then by myself later on. Couldn't find nothing—not even an empty cartridge. That a deputy's star you're wearing?"

"It is. I'm working for John Foreman, the sheriff up at Kingdom City," Lark said and asked the questions he'd put to the other homesteaders. He received the same answers, none of which helped to any extent other than to fortify the belife that the harassment and murders were no part of a scheme to pirate the land.

Starting off toward the lake, visible in streaks and patches through the intervening trees and brush, Lark idly listened to the exchange of talk between Charity and Ford. He had now visited all of the homesteaders, had heard their opinions and considered their ideas—and had gotten nowhere. He was at a dead end, and with no experience in such work, was at a loss as to what he should or could do next. There ought to be a way to draw the killer into the open, force him to show himself—but how? So far every murder committed had been on his terms and at a time and place chosen by him. What he needed, Lark realized, was a plan of some kind to change that—one that would compel the killer to reveal his next intended victim beforehand. Maybe, by using bait—

"Would you like to go on up to Trent's place? It's only a short ways from here."

At Charity Gunderson's question, Prestridge came around, faced her. He gave it thought, shrugged. "Nobody there—nothing to be gained," he said, and glanced toward the sun. "Expect you're wanting to get back home, anyway."

"Yes, stock'll need feeding, and we've got to pick up the girls."

Lark nodded to Frank Ford. "Give my sorrows to your pa. Might tell him that I'll be doing all I can to bring down the man that murdered Earl."

Frank said, "I'll tell him. He's mighty down over Earl. Maybe that'll sort of cheer him up some. So long."

"So long," Prestridge answered as Charity cut the buckboard around and began to retrace their tracks through the brush.

"I've been thinking about your staying in town at Phin Gribble's Bullhead. Like Jim Loven said, getting word to you there if something did happen would take a long time. It'd be better if you were closer—at my place, for instance."

Lark rubbed thoughtfully at the barrel of the rifle across his knees. "Sure an idea worth thinking about."

"You'd be most welcome," Charity said.

Prestridge glanced at the woman. She was looking straight ahead and there was a softness to her features that matched the wistfulness in her voice.

"Can think about it," he said evasively.

The route here, following close to the edge of the lake, was smooth, and the big hoofs of the bay sank deep into the soft, moist soil. Only a thin wall of doveweed, cattails and willows stood between them and the water on their right, but to the left the expanse of undergrowth and trees was dense, and with the sun now swinging lower in the cloudless sky, the shadows were already thickening.

"This is part of Ford's land," Charity said, noting Prestridge's frowning consideration of the ragged area. "Owns more than the rest of us—about twice as much, actually. Still has to clear off this section—aims to do it this fall, I think. Don't know if he will now or not."

"Back home this is what we'd call the brakes," Lark said. "All mesquite, cactus, snakes, rocks and steers that don't want to get caught. Always hated working it—"

The dry crack of a pistol cut through Lark Prestridge's words. As wood splintered from the edge of the buckboard's seat, he reacted instantly. Gripping his rifle firmly, he leaped to the ground.

"Get out of here!" he shouted at the woman. "And don't stop till you get to Loven's!"

17

Holding tight to the Henry, Lark rushed straight for the brush in which he'd seen a spurt of powder smoke. As Charity Gunderson whipped the old bay into a lumbering run, setting the buckboard to swinging from side to side, Lark caught the crackle of dry branches immediately ahead of him.

He threw himself to his right instinctively, expecting a second shot to be fired by the bushwhacker. None came. Suspicious, wondering, Prestridge rushed headlong into the springy growth, hurried on, striving frantically to get a glimpse of the killer.

Nothing. No sound of anyone running, no sign of movement. Lark halted, breathing hard, and stifling the raspy gasps, listened. He should be able to hear even the smallest sound of movement in the sun-withered, dry growth. But it was as if he were utterly alone in the universe.

Prestridge remained for a full ten minutes, thinking the killer had simply hidden himself and was waiting out a time until he felt it safe to move.

But when that period had passed and the rough spread of wild land still lay hushed in the afternoon's heat, he swore deeply, and giving it up, walked slowly back to the road.

The killer had fired a pistol—not a rifle as had been the case in the previous murders. That thought occurred to Lark as he followed the tracks left by Charity Gunderson's buckboard. Could that mean there was more than one killer? If so, such would void the prevailing assumption that the murderer was a kill-crazy lunatic settling a grudge.

He reckoned he'd been too close to the man for him to get off a second shot. Evidently his leaping from the buckboard and charging head on toward the spot where the man was standing had taken him off guard, unnerved him. Startled, he'd turned and ducked deeper into the brush, and managed, somehow, to make an escape.

Had the killer been trailing along, unseen, with Charity and him all afternoon, and then made his move at what he considered an opportune time—there in the wildness of the brakes on Ford's land? It was possible. The feeling that he and the woman were being watched had come to him as they were traveling between—

Lark hesitated in stride as the sound of a running horse coming up to him from the direction of the Loven place reached him. Stepping in behind a tall clump of mock orange, he waited. Shortly the homesteader, astride a big gray, apparently drafted into service on the spur of the moment since he still wore parts of wagon harness, broke into view.

"You get him?" Loven called as Lark moved into

the clear. The man's features were taut and there was hope in his voice.

"Never had a chance to shoot," Prestridge said as Loven drew up beside him. "Ducked into the brush—never did get even a hindquarter look at him."

The homesteader sighed heavily as his shoulders went down. "Can easy see why. That's damned rough country. We all was sure hoping—but ain't no use moaning about it."

Lark started to mention that the killer had tried with a handgun this time instead of a rifle, decided against it. Loven would get the same idea that had come to him—that there was more than one murderer involved—and it was just as well that belief didn't spread. The people along Arabella Lake were worked up enough now without further fueling their jitters with such discouraging information. And there could be no truth in it, anyway. The killer, his intended victim or victims being at close range, could have elected to pass up the rifle, use his pistol.

"Charity said that there bullet didn't miss by far," Loven remarked, patting the broad back of the gray as an invitation to mount and then extending his hand to Lark. "You figure he was shooting at her—or you?"

Prestridge, taking the proffered hand, vaulted onto the horse. "Be hard to say."

"Well, she's one of us homesteaders—and that killer don't know you, does he?"

"Don't think so," Lark said as Loven swung the big horse about and started him back along the road. "Charity get to your place all right?" It had suddenly occurred to him that the killer could have followed her, which would have accounted for his own failure to turn up the man.

"Shook up a mite. Had that old bay running faster'n he's ever done before, I expect. You talk to Linus Ford?"

"Only to Frank."

Prestridge was giving him thought now. The killer had fired on Charity and him only a few minutes after they had left Frank Ford. It seemed strange that the younger Ford hadn't come to investigate the shot. He undoubtedly would have heard the report—not that there were any grounds to suspect Frank. It was said he was asleep in bed at the time his brother was slain.

Prestridge, bracing himself against the solid impact of the gray's trot, glanced up at the sound of voices. Loven's place was just ahead. He could see Charity standing in the yard near the buckboard talking to another woman—Amy, Loven's wife, he supposed.

The sun's rays were slanting into the hardpack, and Charity's red hair was glinting brightly as she moved her head while talking. Seeing Loven and him aboard the gray, she wheeled at once and hurried forward, relief filling her eyes and softening the worry in her features.

"You're all right!" she cried.

"I'm fine," Lark said, slipping off the gray. "Glad you got here without any trouble."

"Did you see who it was?"

Prestridge shook his head, recounted what had taken place. The woman's shoulders drooped. "I—we—Amy and me were hoping and praying that you'd be putting an end to all our trouble—that you—"

"There'll be a next time," he cut in quietly.

Charity glanced up in alarm. "Oh, Lark, I didn't mean—"

"I know what you meant," Prestridge said, smiling, and ducked his head at the buckboard. "Getting late. We'd better be moving for your place."

At once Charity crossed to the vehicle, and waving a hasty farewell to the Lovens, climbed onto the seat. Lark settled down beside her, and snapping the lines, the woman put the bay in to motion.

"I'm glad you're all right," she said when they were underway.

"Same goes for you. Worried some that he might have gone after you."

"Then you think that he was trying to shoot me?"

Not sure. Could just as well have been meant for me. Lucky for both of us that he missed. . . . Forgot to ask you more about that fellow Minton. You said he'd pulled out."

"First thing when trouble started, him and his wife. Never did get to know her. They packed up and went back to where they came from—somewhere on the other side of the Mississippi. Don't think they were much at farming."

"He sell the place or just leave it flat?"

"Did same as Caroline Lockwood—left the papers with Hotchkiss at the general store. Told him if a buyer came along to make a sale and send him whatever he had coming."

Hotchkiss again. . . . Prestridge rolled that about in his mind, but made no comment. He was still trying to piece the bits of information that he'd managed to gather into some sort of pattern when they rolled into Galen Hill's a short time later and picked up Maggie and Mary.

The girls in the buckboard, and Charity's thanks

expressed to Patience Hill—Galen was off somewhere in the fields, she said—they moved on. The sun was now well down toward the rugged horizon in the west, and Charity, using the slack in the lines, endeavored to urge the old bay to a faster gait, but with little success. The big gelding had a mind of his own, and more accustomed to the slow, steady pulling of a plow, he stubbornly refused to be hurried.

"Seeing and talking to the others help you any?" Charity asked as they reached the boundary of Hill's property and entered Lockwood's.

They had discussed the question to some extent earlier, and Lark guessed Charity was only trying to break the glum silence that lay between them, but he gave her an answer, nevertheless.

"Haven't been able to string it into anything that adds up to sense yet," he said.

"I've been thinking," the woman said, a deep frown on her face, "that maybe that killer was hanging around the Ford place hoping to get a shot at either Frank or Linus."

"If he was it's a change. Always before, according to what I've been told, he'd sort of drop out of sight after he'd killed somebody, and lay low for a few days."

"That's true," Charity said, "but what if there's more than one of them? What if he has a partner?"

"If there is it'll mean we're not dealing with a maniac like you've all been thinking. There'd hardly be two of them with a grudge. But I wondered about that maybe being the way of it, too. Whoever it was took that shot at us did it with a pistol. Other times it's been a rifle. Could mean a different man—and could mean the same one just took a notion to use a handgun. . . . That smoke up ahead?"

Charity leaned forward, shaded her eyes with cupped fingers. She stiffened and a wave of fear and anxiety washed over her face.

"It is—and it looks like it's coming from my place!" she cried, and began to whip up the horse.

18

The buckboard rattled and bounced as it raced over the uneven road. Lark, fearing the girls—both clinging tightly to the back rest of the seat—might be thrown from the vehicle, placed his arms about their small shoulders.

"Hang on!" he shouted above the racket. They returned his words with grave, frightened half-smiles.

"It's the barn!" Charity said in a tense voice as they swung around the point of the last intervening spur of brush and saw the yard.

One of the girls began to cry—Mary, Prestridge thought it was—and at once her sister set about consoling her. Charity seemed not to notice, but features pale beneath their tan, bent forward intently, eyes narrowed, she continued to hammer at the lumbering bay for more speed.

"In the barn—the stock!" she said as if reminding herself. "Our cows—and the other horse."

Prestridge came partly erect, the rifle snapping into place at his shoulder. A figure, flaming torch in hand, had come from the rear of a small shed, and as smoke began to spiral up from it, started toward the main house at a fast walk.

Legs spread as he sought to steady himself in the wildly rocking, plunging buckboard, Lark threw a shot at the intruder. At that identical moment the man—slightly built, a dark slicker concealing his body, slouch hat pulled low on his head—caught the sound of the oncoming vehicle. He halted, and as Prestridge's bullet went wide, pivoted and rushed for the cover of the brush.

Cursing, struggling to maintain his balance, Lark levered a fresh cartridge into the Henry, endeavored to draw a bead on the outlaw legging it for the dense brush. The erratic motion of the buckboard made it impossible, but he triggered a second shot nevertheless, choosing a fraction of a moment when he had his sights centered on the man. It was another clean miss, he saw, as dirt spurted from the ground ahead of the man, now plunging into the dense growth.

"Girls—get the water bucket from the house! Bring it to the well!"

Charity was yelling instructions even as she pulled the bay to a stumbling halt. Dropping the lines, she sprang from the buckboard and headed for the barn at a run.

"Got to open the door—get the stock out!" she cried.

Prestridge, rifle still up, was off the seat and on the hardpack as quickly as the woman. He threw a glance toward the lake. The intruder had disappeared into the brush. It would be useless to pursue—and he'd best do what he could to check the spreading flames. Luckily they had arrived on the scene only minutes after the outlaw had set fire to the dry litter and weeds he'd piled against the side of the barn.

Propping his rifle against the wall of the house, Lark snatched up an empty feed sack from a nearby bench, hurried to the well. The two girls had reappeared with the tin bucket used for household water, quickly surrendered it to him when he held out his hand.

Filling it from its wooden counterpart attached to a rope, he lowered the container, allowed it to fill and brought it back up. Setting it on the bench, he jammed the feed sack into it until the coarse fabric was soaked.

"Draw another bucket of water!" he said to the girls, and taking up the filled metal container and the dripping feed sack, started for the barn.

Reaching the structure, Lark sloshed the water against the burning wall a foot or so above the flames. As it trickled down, sizzling and steaming when it came in contact with the flames, he began to beat at the flickering, yellow tongues with the wet sack.

A few yards away Charity Gunderson, the door to the building now open, had driven her two cows into the yard, was turning back to get the horse. The place was filled with smoke; Prestridge could see it seeping through the cracks between the boards and drifting out of the windows and loft vents. He doubted there was any fire inside. Likely the smoke was originating from the wall.

The sack quickly dried, and seizing the tin container, he ran back to the well with both. The girls had managed between them to draw the wooden bucket to the top, and setting it again on the bench Prestridge soaked the sack once more. Pouring what water remained into the other container, he wheeled and returned to the barn. Again throwing the contents of the bucket on the now smoldering wood, he once more set about beating out the last of the glow with the sack.

Nearby Charity had succeeded in getting the horse, a mate to the bay, into the open, was driving him and the cows toward a small corral at the rear of the house, occupied at that moment by Prestridge's buckskin. Elsewhere chickens were clucking nervously, and from beyond the barn came the anxious grunting of hogs, disturbed by the smoke-tainted air.

But the fire was out, leaving only a small expanse of charred planks as a reminder of what could have been a disaster had they not arrived in time. Turning from the bulky structure, Lark put his attention to the small shed that had been blazing furiously while he bent his efforts to the more important building.

"Reckon we've lost that one," he said to the woman, coming up to stand beside him.

She was breathing hard from her efforts. Soot streaked her face, and her hair had loosened, was hanging in wisps about her neck and shoulders.

"Barn and the stock's all that matters," she said with a shrug. "Shed was empty, anyway. Al used it to keep tools in until he fixed a place in the barn." She came about as her small daughters hurried up. "You girls all right?"

Both answered at the same moment, looking shyly at Lark.

"They were a big help," he said, and shifted his glance to the barn. "Except I'd better see if everything's jake inside there. A spark might've floated in."

"I'll go with you," Charity said, and nodding

to the girls, motioned toward the house. "Go set the table, girls. We'll have supper, same as always."

Lark, dropping back, took up his rifle, and carrying also the wet feed sack, rejoined Charity at the entrance to the barn. She was looking off in the direction of the brush into which the intruder had disappeared, and for the first time Prestridge thought he could see fear in her eyes.

Moving by the woman, Lark entered the shadow- and smoke-filled building and crossed to the side where the fire had been set. Getting in close, he felt for heat in the boards while he looked closely for live sparks in the area. The planks felt damp and cool and he could see no evidence of sparks anywhere near the corner. He reckoned everything was safe.

"Probably best you leave the stock in the open until this place airs out," he said as the retraced their steps through the haze to the structure's entrance.

Charity nodded. "Can stay in the corral. Cows won't like it, will probably put up a fuss—" The woman broke off, halted just inside the door. "Lark, are you going to spend the night?"

Prestridge tossed the feed sack into a corner, frowned, stared off toward the lake. Quail were calling softly back and forth in the quiet of dusk.

"Hadn't aimed to—"

"I—I'd like it. Not so much that I'm scared, for the first time, but with you I feel—"

As she hesitated, Prestridge came about, faced her squarely. "You're a mighty fine-looking woman, Charity Gunderson. You can do a hell of a lot better than me," he said, and moved on into the open.

For a long breath she remained motionless and then followed him through the doorway. Wordless, face tipped down, she brushed by him as she hurried for the house.

In that next instant a rifle shot broke the hush of the closing day. Lark Prestridge spun half about, went down full length onto the hardpack.

19

Dazed, a sharp stinging on the side of his head, Prestridge struggled to rise. His arms seemed weighted, utterly devoid of strength, and he could do little more than lift himself a few inches off the packed soil.

He was vaguely aware of Charity Gunderson bending over him briefly, of her saying something, of her picking up his rifle and stepping back. The sudden, quick bark of the Henry then hammered at his wavering consciousness and he realized the woman was firing at the bushwhacker. She had looked first to see if he was badly injured, had recognized that he was only stunned, and seizing the opportunity, opened up on the killer.

Shaking his head, Lark again made an effort to pull himself upright, fighting the weakness in his arms and the fog shrouding his brain. But the mist was clearing slowly and the numbness was leaving. He got to his hands and knees, hung there for what seemed an eternity, and then, sucking in a deep breath, lunged to his feet. Charity, the yard, the barn and the house, and the wall of brush all spun about him sickeningly in an ever tightening circle for several moments, finally came to a stop. He heard the woman's anxious voice.

"Lark! Lark! Are you all right?"

She had laid the rifle aside, apparently having expended its magazine of shells, was looking at him closely. He nodded carefully.

"Just clipped me . . . grazed," he said, touching the burning streak just above his right ear. "Nothing."

The woman's color was high and the flare of excitement, or fear, was in her eyes. "Hardly any blood," she said, making a hasty examination.

He pulled away, and squatting—not daring to bend over—picked up the Henry. Digging into a pocket for cartridges, he began to refill the weapon, gaze focusing unsteadily on the brush where the shot had come from.

"You think there's a chance you hit him?" he asked. A tense hush had settled over the yard now that the crackle of the rifle had ceased, but the sharp, dry smell of powder smoke still hung in the air.

"No way for me to tell," she said. "Saw where the shot came from—that thick patch of scrub oak. Emptied your gun into it when I saw you weren't bad hurt."

"I'll take a look," Lark said, jacking a shell into the chamber of the rifle.

He took a step forward, staggered slightly, balance still off. Immediately Charity caught at his arm.

"Best you wait a few minutes longer."

He pulled clear of her grasp. "I'll be fine," he said impatiently, and continued for the brush.

Prestridge reckoned there was no doubt now who the killer was concentrating on; back at the brakes it had been a question in his mind. The bullet that struck the buckboard could have been for either Charity or him. Now it was clear. They had been together in the yard and the killer had an open shot at each; he'd passed up the woman. That could mean only one thing, and proved earlier thoughts: his identity was known by the killer just as was his purpose for coming to Arabella Lake.

The old, haunting wonder concerning Gabe Hartline came back to mind again. Had the gunman mistaken him for someone else—or had he been waiting there to kill him? If that were true then there was much more to it than the people of Arabella thought. The killer-with-a-grudge idea was out, and some sort of conspiracy involving others was the real answer—with Hartline either being a part of it or merely a hired tool.

Too, there was every likelihood that the person firing the pistol shot back at the brakes on Linus Cord's land was not the same as the one who had just felled him with a rifle shot from the edge of the lake after being interrupted in the process of setting fire to the Gunderson property.

Of course, a man riding hard and fast would be able to cover the distance intervening and have time to get the fires started, taking into consideration the stops Charity and he had made, and the slowness of the old bay gelding. Thus it was possible that only one man was involved—but it was equally logical to believe there were two.

Counting Hartline, that would add up to at least three involved in the murders at Arabella, and—Lark brushed at the sweat on his forehead, smiled grimly—he came damned close to being their latest victim!

Who had set him up? That question dogged Prestridge's mind persistently as he gained the stand of scrub oak where the bushwhacker had been hiding. He still had a deep mistrust of John Foreman, one born of previous association and experience in the war. The man had been no friend of his in those days, and being of an envious, often jealous nature, had demonstrated a capability for vindictiveness on several occasions.

But Foreman, in a bind with the governor of the territory and others well up in the political hierarchy over his failure to capture the killer at Arabella Lake and put an end to the trouble there, would hardly send him down to clear up matters—and have a man waiting to kill him before he could even get started. No, Foreman was much too ambitious to be that stupid, unless—

Lark Prestridge's thoughts came to a full stop; unless John Foreman had even greater, far more reaching plans in mind than politics! He could, either on his own or in league with certain other men, be laying the groundwork for some grandiose scheme that would net a fortune for himself and his partners, if there were others.

It all made sense to Lark. Foreman had been too friendly that day in Kingdom City. Such had aroused his suspicions, he recalled, and then, swayed by the man's cordiality and the offer of a job, he had let it pass.

He had no proof of Foreman's duplicity, Lark realized. He had only suspicions based on acquaintance with Foreman, and he had to admit that during the stress and strain of a war a man was apt to do things that under normal circumstances would never occur to him. He'd keep such thoughts to himself, but in the back of his mind, Lark decided, and he reckoned that ought to apply to his plans and ideas, too; he'd keep them to himself—just to be on the safe side.

Shrugging, Lark began to search around in the stand of oak for signs of blood. He found nothing, and widened his probe. Again he drew a blank—failing even to turn up the place where the outlaw had left his horse. A clever man, he had probably tethered his mount some distance away, thereby reducing the possibility of its tracks being found and followed.

One thing was certain: the bullets Charity had poured into the scrub oak had not found a target. In all likelihood the man had dropped back and was hurrying to his horse by the time the woman had taken up the Henry and begun levering bullets into the brush. Wheeling, Prestridge made his way back to the house.

The good, inviting odor of cooking food greeted him as he entered. The table was set for four, and Charity, her hair a deep, glowing mahogany in the lamp light, met him with a warm smile as he paused and looked questioningly at her.

"You've gone to a lot of work—I aimed to ride on into town," he said.

"No need for you to go before you've had your supper," she replied. All signs of tension had gone from her now. "You can wash up on the back porch. I'll have it on the table by the time you're ready."

Lark's opposition melted. The smell of frying meat, of hot biscuits and black coffee, the air of homey hospitality that filled the house was too much to turn his back on.

Standing his rifle against the wall near the doorway, he crossed through the house to the landing at the rear. There he made use of the water, soap and towel that Charity had provided, and quickly returned. Supper was on the table, as she had predicted, and Maggie and Mary were already in their places. Waiting while the woman brought the pot of coffee and had sat down, Lark took the chair left for him at the head of the table.

At once Charity lowered her head, as did the youngsters, and repeated a short blessing—one familiar but long neglected by Lark. When it was over he glanced up at her.

"This is a real treat. Don't know how I can thank you."

"Maybe there's a way," Charity said frankly as she began to pass the plates of food around. "Did you see any sign of me hitting that bushwhacker?"

"Found where he stood, nothing else. Expect he ducked off into the woods after firing that shot."

"Probably. . . . I've got a feeling he's still out there, somewhere," Charity said, as they began to eat. "I don't know why—and there's nothing for sure, of course—but the feeling's there."

Lark nodded thoughtfully. "Does look like things are coming to a head—the fire, us getting shot at twice, Ford's boy murdered. Be a right good idea for me to take you and your girls over to the Hills' for the night."

"Be a better idea if you'd stay here with us," Charity said. "There's plenty of room, and if nothing turns up you could ride on into town in the morning. That is, you could if you don't have to be there tonight."

Lark was aware of the woman studying him intently, awaiting his reply. The girls, too, had paused, were watching him.

"No, no reason why I have to go back," he said, glancing through the open doorway. The shadows were gathering, but full dark was yet a good hour away.

"Then stay," Charity said. "Please—"

"Might be a smart idea," he said. "Could try pulling a trick on that bushwhacker—if he's still around."

"Trick?"

Prestridge nodded. "Soon as I'm finished with my supper, I'll mount up and head for town. You pull your blinds, do what you usually do to get ready for night. I'll ride far as the first thick brush and stop. When it's full dark I'll double back."

"Come to the side door," Charity said, pleased with the idea. "There's some lilac bushes that'll hide you. Can walk along them, not be seen. I'll leave the door ajar."

"Ought to work," Lark said, resuming his meal. "Once I get inside you can turn down the lamps, go on to bed. I'll watch for the killer. Just could be he'll make another try at burning you out."

"I'll watch with you," Charity said firmly. "It's as much my job as yours. Besides you'll be needing plenty of coffee."

20

The ruse had failed. Either the bushwhacker had seen Lark Prestridge return to the Gunderson house not long after darkness had closed in, or he'd had other plans that took him elsewhere.

In either event, Prestridge had spent the night dozing fitfully while maintaining a watch over the Gunderson property, the long hours alleviated considerably by Charity's presence and a constant supply of her strong and black, if bitter, coffee.

He had ridden out shortly after breakfast, assuring the woman at the time of his departure that he would drop back sometime during the day. He wanted to ask around town if anyone had noticed a rider entering the settlement around dark that previous day, he explained; the killer, perhaps, believing his bullet had scored, and faced with a fusillade of lead from Charity, could have hurried on to Arabella. It was a small hope, but it was something to work on.

"Ask at Yankee Quale's saloon," the woman had suggested. "His is the first place you'll come to when you enter town. Yankee would have noticed. He's the kind who never misses anything."

But the saloonman was of no help. A squat, red-faced man with black eyes and a sly expression, he rubbed at his neck while he considered the star Lark was wearing.

"Weren't nobody come to town from towards the lake," he said. "Not yesterday or today—'cepting you. Recollect seeing you ride out, but you sure didn't come back—not till now."

Quale's tone carried a note of accusation, as if Lark's failure to return were a personal affront.

"Had work to do," Prestridge said, and pivoting on a heel, headed for the door. "Obliged."

Hotchkiss' store was next in line on that same side of the street. Entering, Lark talked to the merchant for several minutes, absently noting while there Reuben Cade emerge from the Bullhead, mount his horse, and ride on. The storekeeper had seen no one, and Lark, hopeful that Martha Cade was also in town, returned to the street, where he crossed over and questioned, in succession, the proprietors of the feed store and livery stable—and learned nothing.

Only mildly disappointed, since he had expected little, and still hoping he would encounter Martha, Lark went on to the Bullhead.

"Was nobody come in here," Phin Gribble said, answering Prestridge's question while he poured a drink.

"Not even any of the folks living in town?"

"Nope, was plenty quiet. Earl Ford getting hisself killed stopped everything cold." The saloonman paused, considered Lark critically. "Looks like you had a close call yesterday."

"Did for a fact," Lark said, and related the incident at Gunderson's where he had all but got a bullet in the head.

Phin Gribble whistled softly, leaned over and examined the welt above Prestridge's ear. "Can't come no closer to buying the farm than that," he observed and settled back. "You get a squint at the jasper that done it?"

"Nope. Bullet knocked me loco for a few minutes. Charity—Mrs. Gunderson—grabbed up my rifle and emptied it at him, leastwise into the brush where she figured he was standing. Didn't hit him. I had a good look around, couldn't find any blood."

Gribble was studying Lark closely. "You and the widow Gunderson sort of got acquainted yesterday, seems. One hell of a woman, I expect."

"She's carrying a big load, but she'll make it if I can get that killer—or the killers—out of the way."

Gribble frowned, said, "Killers? That mean you figure there's more than one?"

"Beginning to think so," Prestridge said. "Saw Reuben Cade come out of here a bit ago. You know if his daughter rode in with him?"

The saloonman shrugged. "Ain't knowing. . . . What're you aiming to do now?"

"Go back to the lake, spend my time riding. If I keep looking—patrolling, I guess you could call it—enough I'm bound to run into some sign."

"Any special place you've got in mind?"

"Patch of scrub oak below the Gunderson place. Was where that bushwhacker was standing when he threw down on me."

"Thought you said you looked, couldn't find any sign—"

"Said I didn't find any blood. Was getting dark

so I couldn't fan out, look for anything else. Planning on doing that today—when I get back."

"As good an idea as any," Phin said. "You want Nellie to fix you up a bite of lunch to take along?"

Lark shook his head, started for the door. "Won't need it. Had a big breakfast."

"And you can always drop by the widow Gunderson's if you get hungry," Gribble said jokingly.

Prestridge shrugged, stepped out into the open. He could, that was certain, but he had a feeling it was the last thing he should do. Charity was becoming a mite too possessive for comfort. Lark halted abruptly, pleasure flowing through him. Martha Cade was coming out of the general store, was smiling at him as she crossed the landing.

"Good morning," she called, descending the steps.

Lark touched the brim of his hat and moved forward into the street to meet her. He was wishing he could put in a better appearance—that he'd taken time to buy the new clothing he needed, but there had been no opportunity.

"Was hoping I would see you," the girl said as they stopped.

She was wearing a corduroy riding skirt, a pale-blue shirt open at the collar to reveal a bit of lightly tanned throat. Glove-leather black boots were on her feet and a flat-crowned plainsman-style hat was set to a jaunty angle on her head.

He grinned hopefully. "There something I can do for you?"

"I—we—my pa and I would like to have you come out to the ranch, spend the day," Martha said hesitantly. "You could take dinner with us—or rather with me—even stay for supper if you like. It will give you a chance to look the ranch over, help you make up your mind about going to work for us—"

Martha broke off, a slight frown crinkling her even features as she noted, for the first time, apparently, the star he was wearing.

"I didn't know you were a deputy sheriff."

"Just for a spell," Lark explained. "I'm trying to get to the bottom of the murders down here, put a stop to them." It was his turn to pause, study her. "Does it make a difference—me being a lawman?"

"Of course not," Martha replied. "It just surprised me. You didn't say anything about it yesterday."

"I've been keeping it under my hat until I got my feet on the ground, sorted folks out a bit."

"I see. . . . Do you think you can manage it, coming out for the day, I mean? Pa will maybe want to talk to you about that job when he gets back. He went to Crawfordsville, and it will probably be around dark before he returns, and I—I—"

Lark waited, wondering what else the girl intended to say. Whatever, Martha elected not to complete her words, instead looked off toward the higher hills beyond the town.

Prestridge gave the invitation thought. Apparently Cade was serious about offering him a job on the Lazy C; just why Lark still could not puzzle out. Never before had he had that kind of good luck. To the rancher he was a stranger, a down-and-out drifter, a saddlebum. Why would a man like Cade take an interest in him?

Could it be that somehow, for some reason, he had impressed the rancher, causing the man to take a liking to him? Some men were that way; quick first impressions counted high with them. Cade could be that kind. Or was it all Martha's doings? Was she behind the offer, pushing her father to hire him? He warmed to the thought.

"Of course, if you're too busy being a deputy—"

Lark heard the girl's words, swore inwardly. He'd like nothing better than to spend the day at the Lazy C in the company of Martha Cade, but he was obligated to stay on the job. Earl Ford's death, the attempt to burn down the Gunderson farm, the shots taken at him all in a space of a few hours when before days had elapsed between incidents, seemed to indicate that matters were drawing to a head. He couldn't very well absent himself right when the homesteaders at Arabella Lake would need him most.

"Maybe, if you don't feel you can spare the time—"

"Not the problem—and I'd sure like to accept the invitation, but—"

"Well, maybe you could ride out around dark and have supper with us, when you're through. You have to eat."

"For a fact," Prestridge said, "and you can count on me being there—if I'm still alive and able."

He paused, eyes reaching past Martha, beyond the town, the trees, to the sky above Arabella Lake. A smudge of dark smoke hanging there was rapidly thickening, growing. Another fire! Who was it this time? Gunderson's again? He glanced at Martha Cade as a thought, a throwback to earlier suspicions of Reuben Cade and Gabe Hartline and the possibility they were somehow involved in the murders, returned to fill his mind.

Had Martha purposely invited him to spend the day on the Lazy C as a means for keeping him occupied, and away from the lake? It was a wild, ridiculous thought, but Lark Prestridge had reached the point where he was grasping for answers, and he passed up nothing.

"Like to ask a question," he said. "Was your pa in on the idea of having me out for the day?"

Martha's full brows lifted slightly, and a puzzled look came into her eyes. "Well, yes, I guess it was both of us. We talked about it at breakfast before Pa left."

Maybe—just maybe—Reuben Cade was mixed up in whatever was going on at Arabella Lake, Lark decided, again glancing at the smoke, now a heavy, dark scar against the blue, but he was damned certain that Martha would not have a hand in it.

"I'll do my best to be there," he said, pointing to the smoke and starting to move toward his horse. "Right now it looks like more trouble down at the lake."

Martha half-turned, glancing at the thickening cloud. "A fire!" she said hurriedly. "I'll go with you. Maybe I can help."

Prestridge nodded. There was no time to spare for argument, and chances were she could be of use.

"Where's your horse?"

"Around back of Hotchkiss'," Martha replied. "You go on—I'll catch up."

21

It was the Minton homestead. By the time Lark and Martha reached the abandoned structures, all were blazing furiously. And it was not alone in its fiery demise.

"The Lockwood place is going up too," Prestridge said wearily, pointing to the boiling smoke on to the southwest.

"It's terrible!" Martha said, her voice barely audible above the crackling flames. "Who can be doing it? The murderer?"

Prestridge shook his head, brushed off a live spark that had settled on his arm. There was some connection, he was certain, but mindful of his resolution to keep his thoughts on the matter to himself even when around those he trusted, he said, "Anybody's guess. . . . We better get over to Gunderson's, see that Charity and her girls are all right."

Martha flung a quick, evaluating glance at him, but said nothing. Raking the sorrel she was riding with her spurs, she hurriedly moved in beside him.

They reached the Gunderson yard, swung toward the front of the house. The place appeared deserted.

"Charity!" Lark called as they pulled up.

There was no response, and cutting the buckskin about, Prestridge raced across the hardpack to the barn. The door was open, and again he shouted the woman's name. The ragged chirping of a cricket inside the structure was his only reply.

The buckboard. Lark saw then that it was missing. Relief flowed through him. Charity had taken her daughters when she had become frightened at seeing the smoke, and gone to one of the other homesteads—Galen Hill's most likely. Wheeling, he loped back to where Martha waited. She met him with an anxious face.

"Are they—" she began, hesitantly.

"They're gone," Prestridge replied before she could voice her fears. "Stock's loose and her buckboard's gone. Expect she loaded up her daughters and headed for Galen Hill's. Like to know just what happened to scare her bad enough to do that."

Martha was again considering him narrowly, her blue eyes deep in thought and speculation. After a moment she said, "You've become well acquainted with Charity Gunderson, I see."

"She took me around yesterday, introduced me to the other homesteaders," Lark explained, looking about. What could have frightened Charity? There was no visible damage of any sort. "Would've got my head shot off if she hadn't been along, most likely."

"I—I suppose you stayed and had supper with her—"

"Yes, I sure did. There'd been somebody trying

to set her place on fire, too. We got here just in time to put out the blaze, keep it from going up."

He could have also told her that he'd come close to taking a bullet in his head, but let it pass. He was not looking for sympathy, and the injury from the bushwhacker's shot was no more than a deep scratch. But it did seem important that Martha know the truth concerning whatever else transpired.

"Spent the night here, sitting by the windows and that door—in the dark. Was afraid that killer, whoever he is, would come back and have another try at burning Charity out—or worse."

Again Martha murmured, "I see," but she let the subject drop there. "Hadn't we better ride on to the Hills', see for certain that Mrs. Gunderson and her daughters are safe?"

Lark did not miss the formal terms in her question or the faint stiffness in her tone. "Yeh, reckon we'd better," he said, and veering in alongside her, struck south for the Hill homestead.

He saw the Gunderson buckboard and the big bay that Charity had hitched to it standing in the yard as they broke out of the brush. Again relief stirred Prestridge. Charity and her girls were all right. As he and Martha Cade nosed up to the hitch rack fronting the house, the door was flung open and Charity, followed by Galen Hill and his wife, Patience, came into view. The homesteader had a rifle in his hand. All halted at the edge of the porch.

"Expect you all know Martha Cade," Lark said, nodding at the girl as he dismounted.

"Oh, yes," Charity said coolly.

Hill smiled, nodded, and Patience, following his example, said, "Won't you step down?"

"Saw the smoke of the fires from town," Lark said, stepping to Martha's side.

He was too late to assist her. She had come off her sorrel easily, gracefully, was walking toward Patience Hill, smiling. Lark put his attention on Charity. She was looking directly at him, a slight frown on her face.

"We went to your place, found you'd left. What was it that made you—"

"I was afraid for the girls," Charity cut in flatly. "Got to thinking my place might be next. I'm leaving them here and going back, keep watch."

"That's Trent's for damn sure!"

At Galen Hill's words, Lark glanced to the sky beyond the lake. Smoke was now rising from that area. All three abandoned homesteads had now been put to the torch.

"Could it be the Fords'?" Patience wondered.

"Too far north for them," her husband stated. "Doubt if anybody can get close enough to Linus' property to set it afire, anyway. Him and Frank's standing guard. So's Loven—and it's what I'm aiming to do. You think you can give me a hand, Deputy? All I've got around here's womenfolk."

"I need him worse than you do," Charity said firmly. "Patience can use a gun. She can help."

"Yeh, reckon you're right," Hill admitted. "Leastwise it'll be even-steven—me and Patience and you and the deputy."

"Isn't there a chance of getting help from town?" Martha asked, speaking up for the first time since arriving.

Galen Hill snorted. "They're all too scared to help—even if they was of a mind to. They're afraid the killer'll turn on them."

Martha frowned angrily. "It seems to me everyone around here—you folks along the lake and the townspeople—should stand together. I know my father would help if I could get word to him."

"Be too late to do any good for Trent's and Lockwood's and the Minton places—not that they count for much," Galen Hill said. "But we could use some men to sort of watch over those of us that's left until the deputy here figures out who it is doing all this devilment and puts a stop to it. We're all so short-handed that we can't—"

"Charity! Your place is on fire now!" Patience Hill cut in suddenly, pointing toward the end of the lake.

Everyone pivoted, followed the woman's leveled finger. Smoke was surging up, hanging in a dark, ugly cloud in the west. There could be no doubt it was the Gunderson homestead.

And there was something else; it lent further credence to his belief that more than one person was involved in the trouble plaguing Arabella Lake. It would not have been possible for the killer, if he was the one behind the fires, to make the ride from Levi Trent's after setting it ablaze as he had just done to Charity Gunderson's, and then put the torch to it, in just mere minutes.

Lark spun on a heel, suddenly aware of the need to act. He might be able to reach Gunderson's in time to save some of Charity's possessions, but more important, the outlaw who had started the fire might still be there.

"I'm going to see what I can do!" he shouted as he swung up onto the buckskin.

"I'm going, too!" he heard Charity say, and then caught the words she flung at Martha Cade. "I'll be borrowing your horse! My buckboard's too slow."

22

There was no hope of saving any of the furnishings inside the house; that was apparent to Lark and Charity when they swept into the yard. The outer walls of the structure, however, were mostly rock, and they would still be standing when the seething flames had done their work. The barn, too, was burning, but earlier Charity had driven the stock into the open, so there would be no loss there.

Dismounting at the edge of the hardpack, beyond the searing heat of the flames, Charity and Prestridge tied their nervous horses to one of the fence rails, and each carrying a rifle, moved to the center of the yard to watch. The air was stifling, filled with the roaring of the flames, drifting bits of ash and glowing sparks. Smoke was like a thick blanket spread over the areas, stilling the birds and all else.

"Won't be hard to rebuild the house," Prestridge said as they halted. "Can start with the walls—they'll be there."

"But everything else is lost," Charity said in a disconsolate tone. "Clothes, our furniture, food—all the things we've saved. There's nothing left—"

The woman's voice broke, and wheeling suddenly, she threw herself into Lark's arms, sobbing violently. He held her close as he did his best to comfort her while within him anger throbbed ceaselessly. Who the hell was behind the murders—the burn-outs? Who was doing it—and why? Why were they, whoever they were, so determined to drive the homesteaders off their land—so determined in fact, they would stop at nothing?

That it was not a case of a crazed killer exacting vengeance and salving a grudge was definite now; even the people around Arabella Lake would have to admit that such belief was no longer valid. It was—it had to be—a conspiracy involving several; but the question of who and why was still unanswered.

Charity disengaged herself from Lark's arms, pulled away from him, dabbing at her eyes with a bandanna as she did.

"Can you manage a place to stay until you decide what you want to do?" he asked. The flames were beginning to die down although the heat was still intense. "I'll fix things up with Phin Gribble at the Bullhead—you could take a room there, but being over a saloon—"

"I can stay with the Hills, I guess," Charity said, wearily. "But the way things are going they may not have a place to live in themselves by this time tomorrow. Oh, Lark, what's going on here—what's happening to us?"

The woman's voice broke again, but this time she did not turn to him, simply stood with her face buried in her hands.

"Wish I could answer that," he replied, after a few moments. "Can't figure a reason no more'n I can find out who's doing it. Got to admit it's got me stumped."

Prestridge's words halted. Placing his arm around Charity's shoulder, he squeezed her arm. She looked at him questioningly.

"There's somebody hiding in those bushes off to the right," he said in a low voice. "Don't let on you see him."

Charity stiffened angrily, but she kept her voice down. "If he's the one who did this—who's been—"

"Maybe you could get help from the other homesteaders," Lark said, voice again at normal level. "Wouldn't take too long to rebuild. Like I said, you've already got the walls, and if each of them could give you a day each week—"

The woman had caught on. "That's an idea!"

"Just about everybodys at that meeting at Galen Hill's," Lark continued. "Probably last the rest of the day. Now would be a good time to talk it over with them."

"There's no use standing around here watching it burn—that's for sure," Charity said. "When we get back to the meeting at Hills, I'll see if I can get some promises of help."

Turning, they retraced their steps to where the horses waited, and swung up onto their saddles. For a long minute Charity Gunderson sat quietly looking at the smoking ruin that had been her home.

"I loved that house," she said finally, and cutting the sorrel about, headed off along the road that led to Galen Hill's.

"What good do you think that'll do us?" she demanded, almost angrily, when they were well away from the yard. "That was the man who set fire to my place—the others, too, most likely. And it just could be he's the killer—"

"Probably is—one of them anyway."

"I could have put a bullet in him, made him pay for what he—" the woman paused, frowned. "One of them—you mean there's several?"

"There has to be," Prestridge said, and gave his reasons why, pointing out, among other things, the impossibility of a man setting fire to the Trent homestead and within only minutes putting the torch to her house and barn, miles away.

"Then why did we go through all that rigmarole about a meeting and fixing up my place? Figured you had a good reason, so I went along—but we could've grabbed him, made him talk."

"Got an idea when I saw him hunkered down in the bushes, listening to us. Wanted him to overhear us talking about a meeting of all the homesteaders at Hill's, going on right now. With everybody there, he'll figure all the other farms are unattended.

"I think he'll hightail it back to whoever else is in this with him, and they'll grab the chance to hit Loven's and Linus Ford's. There seems to be a big hurry on to get whatever they're after here finished up—all these burnings coming at the same time—so there's a good chance they'll swallow the bait."

"And raid the homesteads where they think nobody's home—"

"Right. That'll be Loven's and Ford's. My guess is they'll hit Ford first, it being the place at the end, and the farthest from Hill's, where they'll expect everybody to be. Once they get it burning, they'll probably plan to move on Loven's—only they'll never get the chance. We'll be waiting for them at Linus Ford's."

"A trap," Charity murmured.

Prestridge nodded. "Once we can get whoever's at the bottom of this out in the open, we'll be able to settle with them. All we need is for that jasper we saw hiding and listening back in your yard to carry the word on to his friend—or friends—and with a little luck, he'll do just that. The gun trap we'll have set up at Ford's will do the rest."

"It'll work, just the way you say it will," Charity declared as they continued along the faintly defined road. "I just wish this could have come sooner—before I lost everything—"

"Same here," Lark said. "But I meant what I said back there about getting the others to help you rebuild. They'll pitch in—you can bank on it. And you recollect what Martha Cade said about her pa helping. Expect he'll be proud to send down some of his hired hands—he's got a big crew working for him."

Charity murmured her agreement. Then, "What about you, Lark? Will you be around?"

He shrugged, brushed at the sweat on his face. "Not sure where I'll be," he replied.

The Hill farm came into view a short time later. Lark slowed the buckskin. "I don't want to take the time to stop, do any explaining. I'd best get along, warn Loven and then go on to Ford's—there'll be some getting ready to do up there. I'll be obliged to you if you'll tell Hill what we're doing."

"I ought to go with you to Ford's," Charity said, frowning. "You may need all the guns you can muster."

"It's Hill that needs extra guns. There'll be three of us at Ford's—and we'll be waiting for them, which will give us an edge. If anything goes wrong here, I want you to fire three shots—fast. That'll mean you need help."

Charity nodded. "I understand."

Prestridge started to pull away, again slowed. "One thing more—I'll take it as a favor if you'll square things with Martha Cade for me. Was supposed to have supper with her tonight. This coming up's got in the way."

Charity's lips tightened as she looked off into the distant valley. Smoke clouds still hung in the sky and their drifting shadows were moving swiftly across the green land.

"All right," she said, shrugging, "but it oughtn't need any squaring-up. If she can't understand—"

"She will," Prestridge said. "Luck—"

"Same to you," Charity said, and moved on down the road.

Lark swung away, struck for the Loven place. He was relieved that he'd been able to convince the woman it was best she stay at the Hills'. That she could use a rifle was evident, but he'd as soon not have her involved in a shootout with an unknown number of desperate men, all willing to kill without hesitation.

Raking the buckskin, he put the gelding to a steady lope. He'd best waste no time at Loven's either—take only what was necessary to explain his plan and set up a signal—four shots—in the event he needed help—and then get on to Ford's. He only hoped that both members of the family were there—and that old Linus would not resent too much being made the bait in the trap—and that he would be agreeable.

◎ 23 ◎

Frank Ford halted Prestridge not long after he'd crossed over Loven's property line and was moving through the brakes. Shotgun leveled, big rabbit-ear hammers pulled back, the younger man lowered his weapon only after he'd made certain of the trespasser's identity.

"What're you wanting?" he asked bluntly.

"Got a scheme hatched up that maybe will put an end to the trouble around here," Lark said.

Frank's shoulders stirred with disinterest. "Ain't nothing worked so far. . . . Was that Gundersons' I seen burning?"

Prestridge nodded. "Only yours, Loven's and Hill's are left. Mind riding up to the house with me? Haven't got time to go over what we're doing twice."

Frank gave that a minute's thought, said finally, "I'll get my horse," and pivoting, disappeared into the brush.

They found Linus Ford sitting on a log deep in a thicket, a short distance from the house. The old man had a pistol strapped around his middle and a Sharps rifle across his knees. He glanced up as Lark and his son approached, spat tobacco at a nearby rock and scowled at Frank.

"Told you to keep watch on that trail."

"Just what I been doing, Pa, only the deputy here come along. Says he's got a scheme he wants to talk to you about."

Prestridge felt the old man's small black eyes drilling into him as he considered his son's words. Silent, Lark rode out the moments, letting him make his assessment.

"Deputy, eh?" Linus said after a time. "Had you figured for a lawman when you shot that fellow there in Gribble's. Sure too bad he weren't the killer. My boy Earl'd be alive right now if he hadda been."

"Was sorry to hear about that," Lark said.

"The killer set fire to the Gunderson place, too, Pa," Frank said. "Ain't nobody's farm left now but our'n, Jim Loven's and the Hills'."

Linus again spat. "Kind of got the feeling something big was stirring," he said, wagging his head. "What's this here scheme you've got hatched, Deputy?"

Prestridge, squatting on his heels before the old man, told him of the eavesdropper at Gunderson's, the false information planted, and what he believed would happen next. Linus mulled the words about in his mind for a time, all the while methodically chewing his cud. At last he spoke.

"Might've been smarter had you just grabbed that jasper and we'd strung him up. Maybe he'd done some mighty loud talking when he seen we wasn't funning."

"Could be," Lark agreed, rubbing nervously at

his jaw. Time was passing swiftly. They should be getting ready. "Figured doing it my way we'll bring them all out where we can take a crack at them. It'll end here."

"If we're real lucky," Linus said.

Prestridge ignored the qualification. "Didn't like setting up your place as bait, but it's the first one they'll come to, being at the end like it is."

"Making us bait, that's what you done, Deputy," Linus said, "but I ain't going to fault you none, not if it puts an end to all the killing and hell-raising that's been taking place around here. Where you reckon we ought to do our hiding out?"

"Back at your place—one of us in the house, another'n in the barn and the third man somewhere in between."

"That shed where we keep the seed, Pa—that'll be about right," Frank suggested.

"Expect it would," Linus said, rising. "Well, let's go get set. I got a special welcome waiting for the bastard that killed my boy."

Frank shrugged. "How you going to know which one done it if there's a whole passel of them?" he asked.

"That ain't no problem," Linus replied. "I'll just keep shooting til they're all dead. Right one's bound to be among them."

Leading their horses, Lark and the younger Ford followed Linus back to the house. As he tied the buckskin to a post at the side of the structure well away from the yard lying between the house and the barn, he turned to the old homesteader.

"Been thinking over what you said. The law's got a hand in this, too, Ford. I don't want them all shot down in cold blood. I aim to call on them to drop their guns and give up. Law has the right to hang them for what they've done."

Ford spat. His eyes sparked angrily. "The hell with the law! There ain't never been none around here—not since the first day I homesteaded the land! Them high muckety-mucks running the government ain't never paid us no mind. For all they give a hoot we might as well've belonged to Mexico."

"Now, Pa, don't get started—" Frank murmured.

"You hush up, boy! You ain't growed enough whiskers yet to have a say-so in nothing around here—"

"Earl died for the place, Pa—and I'm older'n he was. Seems that ought to give me a say-so—and I figure we ought to go along with what the deputy wants."

"And I'm saying it's what we want! Damn government ain't never done—"

"They sent me down here," Prestridge said, impatient to get matters organized.

"Sure they did—after there'd been half a dozen killings and a lot of cuss-fire devilment! Where was they when Al Gunderson got bushwhacked? He was the first one that got cut down. Why didn't the sheriff send us a lawman then?"

"Pa, he did send a couple of deputies—"

"Not till after there'd been a couple more shootings—and how long'd they stick around? Not long enough to work up a sweat! We needed help the day Al Gunderson died, and we sent word to that there sheriff in Kingdom City telling him so. Might as well've told the wind for all the good it done—and ended up with us having to write the governor, asking him to prod somebody into doing something.

"This ain't nothing against you, Deputy. You're the first man to show up that's tried to straighten out things down here. But, far as I'm concerned, the law's come too late. I aim to be my own law and do what's needful. Reckon you'll find Jim Loven and that other fellow, Hill, feeling the same way."

"I appreciate what you've been up against," Lark said, "and maybe if I was walking in your boots I'd look at it like you're doing. Only I can't. I swore to uphold the law, and whether it's been unfair to you and the other folks around here or not doesn't change anything. I want all those outlaws alive—at least as many as I can take. I'm asking you both for help in doing it, but I'll go it alone if I have to. . . . Hanging that bunch for what they've done will go a long way towards establishing law in the territory."

"Seems to me we're sort've counting eggs before they been laid," Frank Ford said. "And we ain't even for sure how many's in the bunch."

"You're right," Lark agreed, "but one or ten, the law has to have its way."

Linus Ford, silent, listened and chewed steadily on his cud. His florid features were set and a deep-seated anger glowed in his shoe-button eyes. Abruptly he turned away.

"Reckon we'll see," he said. "Now, Deputy, you find yourself a place inside the house. Frank, best you get in that feed shed. I'll set myself up in the barn loft so's I can see pretty much in all directions. You see me waving my hat, means somebody's coming."

Frank, shotgun in the crook of an arm, a salt sack of extra shells in his hand, started toward the small structure standing midway between the house and the larger barn.

"Your pa going to listen to me about letting the law have those outlaws—or am I going to have trouble with him over it?" Prestridge asked, delaying the younger Ford.

"I ain't for certain what Pa aims to do," Frank answered, halting. "He's mighty bitter about Earl getting killed. Says if the government had done right, he'd be alive, and I reckon that's the gospel truth.

"Them fellows up there running things plumb forgot all about us down here, they was so danged busy looking out for themselves and their friends in the rest of the territory."

Lark swiped at the sweat on his forehead, hung on to his patience. "Said before that's all changed now. Too bad it took several killings to wake up the governor and some of the others to the fact that there's a settlement here—but it did. Thing to do now is for everybody around here to bury the hatchet, accept what happened, and start off right. You take the law into your own hands you'll only make things worse."

Frank stood quietly in the streaming sunlight listening to Lark Prestridge. The skin on his face and the backs of his hands glistened with moisture, and for a time after Lark had finished, he continued to remain silent, listening now to the trilling of a mockingbird in the trees along the edge of the lake. Finally he shrugged.

"Far as I'm concerned, Deputy, I'm siding with you. I figure we all best forget what's happened and let ourselves become a part of the territory now that we've got the chance. But I can't speak for Pa. We'll just have to wait and see what he does when the time comes."

Lark nodded. At least he'd not have opposition from Frank Ford if old Linus bucked him, and that would help. Watching the younger Ford move off toward the shed for a moment, he pivoted, made his way to the house. Opening the door, and flinching slightly at the blast of trapped heat that met him, he propped the thick panel back, and dragging up one of the straight-back chairs placed at a table, seated himself just inside the entrance.

He had a good view of the yard from that point, but of little else. Frank was in a like restricted position, he realized, but Linus, high above the yard in the window of the barn loft, would be able to see anyone coming from all directions but the east—and there was small likelihood of the outlaws approaching from that side.

The old man had deliberately chosen his place of vantage, and that could mean but one thing; he had no intention of cooperating with the law—was planning to mete out punishment to the outlaws according to his own conception of justice.

Lark supposed he could not blame Ford for the way he felt. That section of the territory had been shamefully neglected by the politicians for so long, apparently, that it had become all but a separate area that relied entirely upon itself. Only when the mysterious killer began to strike, and the people found themselves unable to cope, did—

The sound of three shots coming in quick succession echoed distinctly through the warm air. Lark sprang to his feet. It was the signal from Galen Hill's. Abruptly more gunshots—faint poppings like firecrackers on Independence Day—reached him. Waiting no longer, Prestridge rushed into the yard as the truth dawned on him; his plan had backfired.

"They're hitting the Hill place first!" he shouted, running toward his horse. "We've got to get down there—they'll be needing help!"

Jerking the reins free, Lark vaulted onto the buckskin's saddle, and curved sharply back into the yard. Frank had emerged from the shed, and Prestridge could see Linus Ford filling the window of the loft. The old man waved him on.

"You go ahead, Deputy! This could be some kind of a trick. Me'n Frank'll set tight right here till we know for sure!"

There was no time to argue. The hollow reports of gunshots were now a steady, continuing drum-beat—and Hill had only himself and three women to stand off the raiders. He had to get there fast.

24

He had guessed wrong. The raiders had chosen to hit not Ford's place, which was the most remote, but the one where, presumably, the homesteaders were gathered for a meeting. That added up to one thing, Lark realized; the outlaws were of such numbers that they were confident of their ability to take on all of the homesteaders at one time.

The shooting had slowed somewhat, he noticed as the buckskin raced along the narrow road, and he had a quick worry as to the reason. Could Galen Hill have given up so soon? Or had he simply been overrun by the outlaws? Hill had only the women to stand with him, but Charity Gunderson, he knew from experience, was no greenhorn with a rifle. Most likely Hill's wife, Patience, was equally familiar with firearms—a homesteader's or rancher's woman usually was—and he was fairly certain Martha Cade had been taught the use of a gun. Even so, Lark thought soberly, the odds would be against them.

He drew abreast the Loven place, briefly considered stopping and recruiting the man's help. He let it pass. Loven would feel, and rightly so, the same as did Linus Ford; he'd want to look out for his own property. There were times when people scattered along the frontier were compelled to band together for mutual safety, but this was not one of those instances. Here, where each man had established himself in a house of substance, it was a matter of each looking out for himself and his own—at least until the danger was over insofar as he was concerned; then came the time to pitch in and help a neighbor, if there was need.

Prestridge swept on by Loven's, the buckskin running hard over the grassy soil. The gunshots had picked up, were increasing, and he reckoned Hill and the women were holding their own.

Lark shifted on his saddle, and brushing aside the sweat misting his eyes, glanced down at his gun belt. The loops were filled. He had an ample supply of cartridges for his pistol. He reached down, checked the rifle shells he'd earlier stuffed into his pants pocket. There were a few, but not near as many as he would prefer to have in reserve. He had a bandolier near full back at the Bullhead with his belongings, but he'd not troubled to hang it over his shoulder when he rode out for a look at the country that previous day. More than likely he'd be regretting that bit of carelessness before sundown, he thought, grimly.

As he drew near to Hill's, the firing became even heavier. He'd best see how the land lay, he decided, before riding in, and swinging wide of the structures, Lark sent the buckskin to the crest of a knoll close by that would afford him a view of the yard and its buildings.

Smoke and dust hung over the hardpack in a

shifting cloud. He could see several riders whipping in and out, shooting at the main house where Hill and the women were maintaining a steady return barrage from the doors and windows. So far none of the raiders had been downed. He guessed that was because they were managing not to expose themselves too recklessly.

There were other outlaws in Hill's barn. Lark saw puffs of smoke coming from the partly open double doors as well as from the small, separate tack room in the corner of the building. There appeared to be several men in there, but the shooting was coming mainly from the riders and from behind the large double doors. Altogether he could see seven raiders—but just how many were inside the barn he had no way of knowing.

Hill and the women wouldn't be able to hold out much longer, that was certain. So far their shooting was ineffective, and chances were good they'd soon run out of ammunition. That belief, likely, was what now kept the raiders from charging the house and applying a torch, which undoubtedly they planned to do. They would simply wait, bide their time until it became apparent that Hill and those with him—the other homesteaders, they believed—could no longer muster any resistance, and then make their move.

If that was to be prevented he must act quickly. Already the shots coming from the house were more spaced, as if Hill had given the order to fire more slowly. Lark glanced at his pistol, making certain it was in its holster. Lifting the rifle, he levered it partly open and checked the load in the chamber. Then, snapping the weapon closed, Prestridge spurred the buckskin into motion, circling wide to come in to the barn from the rear. From the back he—

Abruptly the double doors of the structure burst open. A half-dozen more raiders, bent low over their saddles, guns in hands, spurted into view. Two more came from around the far corner of the hulking barn, three from the near. All, weaving and whipping back and forth, rode straight for the house.

Prestridge changed directions at once. He'd have to forget entering the barn from the rear, do what he could to stop the rush on Hill and the women forted up in the house. With the buckskin going downgrade in plunging leaps, Lark raised his rifle, triggered a shot at the nearest rider. The man jolted, fell from his saddle.

At almost the same moment two others in the ragged line of charging raiders buckled, slid from their horses as bullets from the house met them coming on. Yells went up as dust and smoke began to swirl in a thickening cloud over the hardpack.

No one seemed to have noticed him, Lark realized as he came off the low hill, and shortly, after reaching level ground, he swerved into a windbreak stand of brush. He did not slow, however, but, roweling the buckskin, raced on.

A thought had come to him. The men he could see through the dusty glass window of the tack room were taking no chances on getting hit by a bullet—were, except for an occasional shot, leaving it up to the men on horseback now circling the main house, firing indifferently at its doors and windows as if taunting those trapped inside. Undoubtedly they were the ones behind the murders, the burn-outs and all other trouble at Arabella

Lake; the raiders carrying the attack were probably no more than hired gunmen.

If he could get into the tack room, take the men by surprise, he could, by holding a gun on them, force them to call off their killers. There was no side door to the room they were occupying, but there would be one inside the barn—one could gain access to by slipping through a window. He would have to act fast, however, he realized with a tightening in his throat; the slackening in shots coming from the house warned him that Hill and the women wouldn't be able to hold out much longer.

Prestridge reached the yard at the lower end of the barn. The raiders and the main house were now to his right. He could see several horses with empty saddles wheeling about in the haze hovering over the hardpack, evidence that the shots coming from the house had not all gone for nothing.

The window in the wall of the barn was just ahead. Lark pulled the buckskin to a halt, left the saddle in a long jump. Rifle in hand, he thrust a leg through the opening and drew himself into the shadowy structure. Pausing for a moment, he glanced about, getting his bearings. The tack room was half the length of the barn to his right—and there was a door, closed but available. Bent low, Lark ran the short distance to the sectioned-off corner, halted. Hammer back on the Henry, he took a deep breath, raised a booted foot and drove it against the flimsy panel. It gave with a crash and Prestridge lunged into the room.

He had a glimpse of three men wheeling from the window in surprise, but instant recognition was blurred as one came about fast with a pistol, fired, missed. Lark triggered his rifle. As the man slammed back against the wall, the others jerked away—one opening the door to the yard and rushing out, evoking a flurry of shots from the house, the third man dodging off into the murky depths of the barn.

Shocked, Prestridge stared at the upturned face of the dead man lying on the dusty floor. It was Ed Wheeler, the Territory Land Office man. He'd met him that day in Kingdom City. And the one who had sought escape into the yard—that had been Jesse Cahoon, the deputy U.S. marshal. It was hard to believe they had been behind the murders and trouble at Arabella Lake, but they were. And the third man . . . Suspicion flared through Lark as he wheeled to the door in the adjacent wall of the tack room, crossed, and hunched low, began to probe the darkness with narrowed eyes.

Could it have been John Foreman? Considering the identities of the two other men, it was entirely possible. He hadn't gotten a look at the man—the pistol shot, the blast of his own rifle, the smoke and confusion as Wheeler went down, all combined to prevent his seeing who he was. But the odds were all for it being Foreman.

He could see no movement inside the barn, but he was not misled. The man, whoever he might be, was there, waiting, ready to kill him the instant he showed himself. Lark shook his head, smiled grimly. He'd not make it easy for him.

Aware suddenly that the shooting in the yard had ceased, he pivoted on a heel, and still low, doubled across the room to the shattered door through which he had come. With luck, the killer would be watching the other entrance. Pausing long enough to gather himself, Prestridge abruptly plunged through the opening and legged it for the thick timbered side of a nearby stall.

A pistol flared from the darkness on beyond it. Prestridge heard the solid thud of the bullet as it buried itself in the wall behind him. He was caught in the open, at the mercy of the man crouched behind a wooden cask. Heedless, Lark rushed on, levering and firing the Henry as fast as he could work the mechanism while running directly at the cask.

It was the war all over again—charging enemy lines, facing direct fire, ignoring the smoke, the sharp smell of burnt gunpowder, the faint, chilling whirr of bullets passing too close . . . And then suddenly it was finished. No more shots came from behind the cask.

Prestridge stood motionless in the smoke-filled barn, sucking deep for wind. When his breathing had quieted he moved forward slowly, cautiously, rifle ready for instant use. A stride short of the cask he saw the lifeless figure stretched out behind it, stepped hurriedly to its side. Reaching down, he took the body by the shoulder, rolled it over.

It was Phin Gribble.

25

"That's what it was all about," Galen Hill said.

Prestridge, standing with the homesteader in the doorway of the barn, looked out into the yard. The dust and smoke had disappeared, the shock of discovering the identities of the men behind the murders and trouble at Arabella had worn off, and a sort of lethargy had claimed him, leaving him dull and empty. It had been that way for him in the war; death had always left him with a sense of loss, even where strangers were concerned.

Jim Loven had put in his appearance, as had the Fords once it was certain their property was in no danger. Together they had taken charge of the gunmen, those who had not made a hasty departure when they realized that matters had gone against the men who had hired them, and locked them in Hill's feed barn. The ones who had been killed, along with Phin Gribble, Wheeler and Jesse Cahoon, they laid in a wagon and threw a canvas over them. Lark had directed they be taken to Crawfordsville for proper burial; the outlaws were to be delivered to the marshal there, also, where they would be held for John Foreman.

"They had a real fancy scheme cooked up to make the lake a big watering hole for the trail herds. Aimed to take over the town, too," Hill said. "We got it all out of that marshal before he died."

"How?" Prestridge asked. Jesse Cahoon didn't strike him as being a man who'd break down and bare his soul, regardless of circumstances.

Hill cocked his head to one side. "You being the law, and such—you sure you want to know?"

Across the yard Martha Cade, with Charity Gunderson and Patience Hill, had come out onto the porch, were in conversation. Martha raised her hand to him, smiled.

Lark responded, put his attention back on Galen Hill. "Can't see as the law has anything to do with that."

"Probably wasn't fitting," Hill said, "but anyways, we told him he was dying. Had three bullets in him. Me and the ladies nailed him good when he come busting out of that door. Told him we wanted the truth. Told us we could go straight to hell. Right then old Linus Ford steps up and tells him he'd best talk if he wanted burying, otherwise—"

"Otherwise," Lark prompted when the man hesitated.

"Otherwise we'd not bother, we'd just feed him to the hogs. That brought him to terms mighty quick. Got to talking so that we couldn't stop him. Told us everything we wanted to know."

It had been a deal involving Wheeler and Cahoon in Kingdom City, Phin Gribble in Arabella, and a high official of the railroad. They had arranged, through the official, to get the railhead some thirty miles to the south of Arabella moved and re-established a short distance east of it. Cattle coming up for shipment would thus be forced to trail farther and would arrive badly in need of water. Arabella Lake would be waiting to supply their needs.

"They aimed to charge a dime a head for watering and grazing, more if there was a dry spell on. They figured with all the herds being drove up for loading, they'd get rich plenty quick."

"Which they would," Lark agreed. Pulling off his hat, he ran fingers through his thick hair, damp with sweat. "Can see how Wheeler, having an in with that railroad man and knowing the country, could come up with a scheme like that, but the marshal—"

"His part was to furnish the hard cases to do all the hell-raising—and shooting and driving us off our land by one way or other. Seems none of them had the cash to do any buying, so they had to turn to scaring us off. Being a lawman, it was easy for that marshal to bring in the kind that wouldn't back away from killing, and still not do any talking about it."

"Like Gabe Hartline. He was working for them. Had been all the time."

"Yeh, was him that murdered Gunderson and the others—except Earl Ford. The marshal shot him."

"Except it was Cahoon that sent word to Gabe telling him I was on my way and to take care of me when I got here. Can see that now. What I can't see is how Phin Gribble got mixed up in it, and why."

"Me neither," Hill said, shrugging. "That marshal didn't talk much about him. My hunch is Phin was starving to death in that place of his."

"Understood from him that business was good until the murders started and everybody got scared off."

"That ain't so. Phin never did do no good. Went and built his place way too big for the number of folks that'd be patronizing it. I think he was figuring that with the lake turned into a big watering hole for the cattle on their way to the railroad, he'd make a pile of money from the drovers while they was laying over. I'll say this for Phin, he was a lot smarter'n I thought he was. Sure fooled everybody around here."

"Including me," Prestridge muttered, shaking his head. "I guess Gabe Hartline was sort of reporting to him all along, and getting his orders."

"While he was letting folks think he was working for Reuben Cade."

"Cade thought that, too," Lark said. "But it's all done with now. Folks around here can go back to living and farming the way they used to."

"For sure," Hill said. "What're you planning to do—keep on being a deputy?"

Lark raised his glance to the porch again. The women were still conversing busily. Where once he could awaken each day and look forward to nothing, he now found himself faced with making a choice from three ways of life: a job with John Foreman—one that could lead to higher things; one with Reuben Cade on the Lazy C—the kind that was not only to his liking, but there would be Martha and the prospect of their friendship developing and growing into more; and there was Charity Gunderson, a fine, full-blown woman who needed him.

But Lark Prestridge reckoned he'd already made up his mind, although he hadn't been aware of it until that moment.

"I'll be signing on with Reuben Cade at the Lazy C," he said. "Expect I'd better get out there and let him know I'm taking the job—after I tell Martha. She comes first with me from now on, in everything."